Skin Food

First published as an ebook in October 2017

First paperback edition published in January 2021

Published in Miami, Florida, by Type A

Library of Congress Control Number: 2020919404

ISBN: 9780578591230 (paperback)

ISBN: 9780692976876 (ebook)

Written by Type A (Alejandro Callirgos)

SKIN FOOD

TYPE A

Acknowledgements and Dedication

Much love and gratitude to Heezy Yang, Tony Lumina, Markus Obrist, and my brothers—Diego, Rico, and Carlos—for spotting my blind spots.

∞

To Mamama María Antonieta Casanova Lenti, who made me believe that writing is in the blood.

I

"Here we are," Tyson said with a sparkle in his eye, "the world's best airport."

"According to whom?" Lana asked, unconvinced.

"According to the internet. And just look around." He motioned with his hands.

"All airports are the same, really," she said, staring out the slanted windows. "But it sure is nice out."

"Picture perfect," he agreed.

Tyson stroked Lana's lower back as they strolled along the concourse. They felt at ease and grateful for this, their first trip together.

He slid his fingers off her side and reached into his back pocket. He had an imaginary microphone.

"Folks, we have some fantastic weather out there. Winds are coming out of the southwest with plenty of sunshine. Our expected high today is twenty-seven degrees with no rain. Evening plans are looking pretty good as the temperature should drop to twenty-two degrees."

Lana elbowed him on the side. "You're such a goof."

"I didn't even get to the fog," he protested.

"And Celsius, really?"

"I did my homework."

Lana and Tyson followed the Arrivals signs through the moving walkways, taking in the mountain scenery and ignoring the poster advertisements along the way. After some people watching— standing in the Immigration line—they received their passport stamps.

[REPUBLIC OF KOREA]

Lana thanked the immigration officer, and she and Tyson took the down escalator.

{buzz} {flash} A red siren went off, and the conveyor belt was set in motion. Tyson swung their bags off the carousel. His: Black polyester with a black bag tag. Hers: Polycarbonate and kaleidoscopic. Easy to spot.

A restless crowd of people waited on the other side of customs, intermittently holding up signs, fanning themselves, and checking their smartphones. Tyson scanned the signs, some in English but most in Korean.

"Where's our welcome?" he asked.

"I come bearing gifts," a voice said from behind them. Tyson and Lana turned around to see Sam smiling, holding up three grenade-shaped bottles of banana milk. They gave him a group hug and touched his cheeks.

"What?" Sam asked, trying not to blush.

"In college, you only shaved on weekends," Lana said. "It was kind of backwards."

"Today is Friday." He laughed. "And I have a real job now. Priorities and responsibilities."

"You've changed a lot in two months," Tyson teased.

"C'mon," Sam said, rolling his eyes and half-hiding a smile. "How was your flight?" He took Lana's luggage.

Sam seemed like a new man, happier. Maybe it was only natural. He'd left Korea when he was two and had finally made his triumphant return to the motherland. Tyson and Lana were his first visitors.

"So how do we get to your place?" Lana asked when they walked through the automatic doors.

"It's a straight shot on the subway."

"Do you drive?" Tyson asked.

"No need. Public transportation here is a godsend."

One hour, seven subway stops, and three banana milks later, they arrived at Sam's *officetel* in Hongdae. The loft was clean, efficient, and—after the day's travel—thoroughly inviting. They agreed to take a nap before going out.

∞

Steve had had dark days before. Days when he wanted to sit alone in silence. Days when he wanted to veg out in front of the TV. Days when he wanted—no, needed—to drink drink after drink. Today had been especially bad. His sweat was cold, and his heart was beating a kilometer a minute. He was already in a state of shock, so {guzzle}{guzzle} would an energy drink be any more of a shock to his system? He put down the can, closed his eyes, stroked his hair, and dizzily stood up. A shower was out of the question. His friends were lucky he was even going out. They were lucky that Korea had instilled in him a sense of social obligation. He tossed his work shirt on the floor and rummaged through the closet for his least wrinkled button-up. His pants from the night before didn't smell too smoky. Recycling day, he decided. He was mid-pee in the kitchen sink when he heard his change rattling on the coffee table. {zip} He stumbled over to see "Sam" on caller ID.

"Yo."

"Hey. You on your way?"

"No, I just got home from work. One of my…"

"Wha-why'd you work so late?"

"This is Korea, and one of my co-workers died." Steve didn't mince words.

"Uh, whoa."

"Yeah, I still can't believe…" he trailed off with a lump in his throat.

"I'm sorry to hear that. Are you okay? You wanna talk about it? If you don't feel like going out…"

"I can use the distraction."

"Okay. I'm with Tyson and Lana. They're excited to see you. You need anything? Coffee?"

"I just had an energy drink."

"You're ahead of the curve," Sam said. "When do you wanna meet? 10:30?"

"All right. See you at Exit 9."

Steve slid his phone into his left pant pocket and flinched. The cut on his wrist was infected and hurt like all hell. But the shot of pain made him feel awake again, alive.

∞

"One of Steve's co-workers died," Sam told Tyson and Lana.

"Were they close?" Lana asked.

"I'm not sure. But he seems a bit shaken up."

"Does he still wanna go out?" Tyson asked.

"Yeah. He can use some fresh air."

"Attaboy, Steve!" Tyson said.

Lana shook her head in disapproval. Tyson had a lot of growing up to do. He always did.

When they first met, he wore a French Quarter t-shirt and shaggy, unkempt hair. He was pouring a glop of ranch dressing on a paper plate of microwaved pizza rolls, which he washed down with a dark beer and a multivitamin. It was 10:00 a.m. the Tuesday of exam week, and he was in his natural habitat. Tyson was roommates with Sam, and Sam was classmates with Lana. She was at their apartment to work on an economics project.

Sam and Tyson met in the dorm their freshman year at the University of Miami. They played on the same intramural football team and became fast friends over a few satisfying but unspectacular meals at the dining hall. Their shared love of The Rat Pack solidified their friendship. So much so that when they rented an off-campus apartment the following year, they named it The Rat's Nest.

Steve was Sam and Tyson's resident assistant (RA) their freshman year. He was hands-off, to say the least. After he gave a brief orientation speech to his floor ("If you feel homesick yada yada"), he was rarely around. He engineered his life around engineering, spending many an hour in the library stacks and getting hands-on experience in the lab.

In early spring, Steve had a budget for an RA group activity. While other groups had a beach picnic at Crandon Park or attended a Miami Hurricanes baseball game, he opted for a classic fifth grade-style pizza party in the dorm lounge. Most students ate a couple of slices and retreated to their rooms with a can of soda; Sam and Tyson split a pepperoni pizza and got to know Steve.

Steve was a figure of intrigue to Tyson and Sam, like a summer camp counselor is to curious campers. Campers know that their counselor womanizes and gets wasted on weekends, but they can't prove it and the counselor never drops his veil of authority. So Sam and Tyson asked a lot of questions, and Steve answered a few. Over time, the tiny bits of information they collected constituted a very real friendship.

When Steve went to graduate school on a Korean government scholarship, Sam and Tyson vowed to visit him. Three years later, Sam arrived in Korea. Tyson and Lana touched down two months later.

∞

"Light of my life, come here!" Tyson greeted Steve outside Hongik University Station. He embraced him in a long hug, his heavy cologne filling Steve's lungs. "I want you to meet Lana."

"*Encantado*," Steve said in his suavest Spanish.

"*Sí, encantada*." Lana smiled. "We finally meet."

"This must be surreal for you," Tyson said. "When you were our RA, did you ever think that one day we'd be hanging out in Korea?"

"No. Never." Steve smiled, charmed by the question. He shifted his gaze back and forth between Sam and Tyson. They were now his equals.

"What's it like living here?" Lana asked.

"It's all right," Steve replied. "It's comfortable and convenient. The–"

"Do you two hang out a lot?" Tyson interrupted.

"Almost every weekend," Steve said. Sam nodded in agreement.

"Where do you go?"

"Here," Sam said, "and sometimes Sinchon, Itaewon, and Gangnam. The areas with the best bars and clubs. Hongdae is tops. Sinchon has too many students, Itaewon too many expats, and Gangnam too many gold diggers and playboys."

"Will you listen to him?" Steve asked Lana and Tyson. "Sam was such a nice guy in undergrad. He was in the business fraternity.

He volunteered. He played sports. He studied at the library. Now all he does is chase skirts."

Sam cocked his head and shrugged.

"Shall we eat?" suggested Lana.

∞

Korean BBQ. Sam cooked; Steve wasn't hungry. Sam poured beer; Steve was thirsty. This was normal behavior for Steve. He often vetoed anything and everything but alcohol.

"Are you fasting again?" Tyson asked Steve.

"I've never fasted," Steve said matter-of-factly. "What good would that do?"

"Maybe North and South Korea would reunite."

"Doubtful. I think that'll be decided by a game of *kai-bai-bo*," Steve said, tapping his fist to his palm. "Rock-paper-scissors. That's how they do everything in this country."

"You know, you seem to have a knack for living near communist dictatorships. First Cuba and now—"

"And you seem to have a knack for instigating," Steve snapped, his face flushed with anger. He paused and lowered his eyes. "Sorry, I've had a hard day."

The table got tense, and Tyson felt terrible. How could he be so insensitive?

Between bites of barbecue, Sam and Tyson looked at each other, each waiting for the other to ask Steve about his day. It was Sam that Steve told about his dead co-worker, so...

"You wanna talk about it?" Sam asked.

"What?"

"What happened at work."

"No, not now."

A dead end.

The friends sampled the side dishes and pecked away at the egg moat—a crispy mixture of beaten eggs, kimchi, bean sprouts, and green peppers—wrapped around the grill. They ordered more *galmaegisal* and marinated pig skin.

Sam broke the silence. "Guys, get this! We went from pigskin to pig skin." He made a throwing motion.

"Psshh. It's not like we don't have pig skin in Miami," Lana said. "*Chicharónnes*? Cracklings? Pork rinds?"

"Yeah, but this skin is different. It's more chewy than crunchy, and it's better for you. In Korea, every food is good for a kid's height, a woman's skin, and a man's stamina. Or so they say." He chopsticked a square of skin off the grill and dipped it in bean powder.

Steve let a smile slip out, and Sam offered up a round of soju.

"*Geonbae*!"

"Cheers!"

"*Salud*!"

Lana and Tyson's faces cringed, and Steve and Sam laughed. Soju was an acquired taste. One shot of the rice liquor was enough for Lana. But not for Tyson. A couple of little green bottles later, he asked, "Woo, where can we find this stuff in Miami?"

"The bigger liquor stores," Steve said. "But at a premium. Soju is cheaper than water here."

∞

Loaded up on liquor, Sam, Tyson, Lana, and Steve hit the streets of Hongdae. Youthful exuberance. Countless bars and clubs. Street drinking. Fashion. Buskers and beatboxers. Even more countless coffee and cosmetic shops. Egg tart, popcorn chicken, and kebab stands. Makgeolli Man. A Siberian Husky next to a cotton candy machine.

"We're in college again!" Tyson declared.

"This place has a good vibe," Lana observed.

"Zen?" Steve asked Sam.

Steve led the group through the crowds and down a flight of dark and smoky stairs, the beat banging louder with every step they took.

Tyson's eyes doubled in size when they entered the bar. A packed dance floor. A killer DJ and sound system. A pole on a dance platform. Bartenders dancing in sync. Multi-colored, illuminated liquor bottles lined up like a kids chemistry kit. Thai buckets and cheap tequila shots. Red flashing beacons. Just the right amount of strobe lighting. A fog machine so thick they could taste it. A graffiti mural of a six-armed Hindu god of a DJ. Altogether average compared to the models and bottles of Miami that Tyson was used to. But these people were inviting. Girls smiled and guys high-fived him. Arms stretched out to pull him up on stage. Strangers squeezed on the dance floor. Tyson was ready to revel with this new crowd. Then he looked back at Lana and sensed her hesitation.

Steve bought the first round of drinks, Jack and Coke. "What's a weekend without whiskey?" he asked.

Sam got the second round, gin and tonic. Lana ordered vodka shots and Tyson four buckets of Long Island Iced Tea. Soon, the friends lost track of the drink count and one another.

For Sam, time became a blur, an afterthought. The music had him high and the liquor loose. He wasn't caught in a whirlwind; he was the whirlwind, swinging around in circles. When he spotted Tyson standing by the bar, he spun over to him and asked, "How much am I paying you for babysitting?"

"Huh?"

He tapped Tyson's glass with his fingernail. "How much am I paying you for babysitting your drink? The ice is melted."

"Oh." Tyson laughed. "I'll get another."

"You're not yourself tonight."

"You mean I'm not much of a wingman?" Tyson asked.

"Yup, you're not mingling at all. Where's Lana?"

"She went to the restroom."

"So are you two together?"

"Yeah, as of last week."

"You always did say she was like a sister, and we both know how that usually turns out." They laughed.

A couple of Sam's dance partners waved at him in passing. They were unattractive and not just by Miami standards.

Tyson asked Sam, "Why are you wasting your time with those girls? Are you getting community service hours for hanging out with them?"

"Nope. I have yet to volunteer abroad," Sam joked back.

"Those girls are fours."

"Add them up and they're an eight."

"I don't think it works that way." Tyson paused. "Nope. Definitely not. By that logic, if you have two fives, then you have a ten. There's no such thing as a perfect ten. And if you add up sixes, sevens, eights, nines… that's more than perfect. An impossible goddess."

"All right, all right. Enough with the math."

Tyson pointed to a girl dancing on stage. "Look up. She's been eyeing you all night."

Sam had been checking her out, too. She had a beauty mark beneath her right eye, and her waist-hugging white blouse accentuated her curves—or what Koreans call the *s-line*. She mouthed the words to the music and appeared to dance only for herself.

Sam had had the opportunity to dance with several girls that night. Some pretty, some pretty unusual. But he always ignored their advances when she was in sight. He didn't want to ruin any potential chance with her. Now was his moment. They made eye contact, and he jumped on stage.

They danced a bit and Sam played it cool. He had soju to thank for that.

"*Ireumi mwoyeyo*?" he asked in his American accent.

"You can call me Mimi," she responded in English.

He looked up at the ceiling in thought. "Like the Korean Barbie doll," he said. "You can call me Sam, like the Korean... um... What do you drink?"

He hopped off the stage and held out his hand for her.

For the better part of the night, Sam and Mimi got to know each other at the bar and on the dance floor.

He: a twenty-three-year-old college graduate working as an elementary school English teacher. His mother was Korean and his father American. They'd met when his father was stationed at Osan.

She: a twenty-one-year-old biology major. She was born and raised in Ilsan, and she lived with her parents, as is typical in Korea.

"Do you speak Korean?" she asked.

"Not nearly enough. I'm working on it. How'd you get the name Mimi?"

"My aunt called me that when I was little. My real name is Mikyung."

She liked that he danced like he didn't care. They were hopping and grinding to Pitbull when Mimi's friend tapped her on the shoulder.

"Mimi, it's two o'clock. You're drunk. Let's go home," she spoke in grave Korean. Mimi brushed her off. Pitbull said not to stop the party.

"Don't mind her. She's kind of a prude. I think she feels guilty partying this late," Mimi said to Sam.

But her friend was right. Mimi was suddenly sleepy and couldn't keep up with the beat of the music, her rhythm reduced to sloppy swaying. They went to the lockers to get gum out of her purse.

"You want some?" she asked, holding up the pack of peppermint.

"Sure."

"Do you want a whole stick or half a stick?"

"No one's ever asked me that." He paused. "Half a stick, please."

He laid the half stick on his tongue and crushed its half wrapper into a tiny silver ball. Then he flicked the ball into a dark corner. Taking in his surroundings, he saw a couple making out against a wall, ATM receipts scattered on the ground, and his shoes caked in black sludge. People started bumping into him left and right, and he could feel his agitation building. He suggested they go outside for fresh air.

This was the moment of truth. He and Mimi were ascending from the cave and there was no neutral lighting, no smoke and mirrors. The grand reveal. Even with her sleepy face, Mimi was still stunning. Maybe more so because of it. She didn't look as fierce as when they'd first met. Her guard was down.

They sat on a bench outside of Zen, and she rested her head on his right shoulder—but not before getting a glimpse of his eyes. They were a little bloodshot but trustworthy. She spit her gum on the street and dozed off, unbothered by the smoky and sweaty smell of his v-neck.

Sam had expected to chat with the sleeping beauty, and he soon grew tired of random guys pointing at Mimi and giving him thumbs up of approval. He closed his eyes, and a game unfolded around him. Which unlucky pedestrian would step on Mimi's gum? Would it be the Korean guy in black Air Force 1s, the English lad in sand suede Clarks Desert Boots, or maybe the Korean high schooler in silver and pink Nikes? Feet shuffled around the gum. Got one! White gum on white sneakers.

"Damn it!" Tyson said, scraping his Chuck Taylors on the curb.

Sam opened his eyes. "Ready to call it a night?" he asked Lana.

"For a while now. We couldn't find you," she replied.

"Why didn't you just call me?" Sam asked with his thumb to his ear and his pinky to his mouth. Lana and Tyson didn't have their phones and didn't find his joke funny.

"I'll call Steve." Sam was careful not to wake Mimi as he squeezed his phone out of his pocket.

"Did you ever ask him what happened at work?" Tyson asked.

"I didn't get a chance to," Sam said with the phone ringing. "We were walking around the bar, and Steve disappeared. Sometimes we lose each other for hours at a time. One night he took a nap on the street— on a cardboard box in an alley—and called me when he woke up. We always reconnect." Steve didn't pick up.

"Ah well, he's a big boy. We'll see him tomorrow," Tyson said.

"Mimi," Sam whispered as Tyson finished getting the last of her gum off his shoe. "Mimi." He tapped her shoulder. Then he gently shook her. She was in a deep slumber.

"Dude, did she blackout?" asked Tyson.

Sam mouthed an expletive and stared into space. Again, he tried shaking Mimi awake, without success.

"I saw this in a K-drama. Actually, a few of them," Sam explained to Lana and Tyson. "Hopefully she wakes up before we make it back to my place." He picked Mimi up and put her on his back, piggyback style. She didn't flinch, and her facial expression didn't change. "Can you get her purse?" Sam asked Lana.

"When's the honeymoon?" Tyson asked Sam a ways down the road.

"I should be asking you lovers."

"You told him?" Lana asked Tyson.

"Yes, love."

She stuck out her tongue in playful disgust.

"So how did you two get together?" Sam asked.

"As you know, we took Summer Session together…" Lana started.

"Right."

"Well, one day after class we went to a café in Wynwood. To study. We were there maybe five, six hours and had only ordered a couple of drinks…"

"Non-alcoholic," Tyson clarified with his index finger pointed up.

"When the server put a tea light at the end of our table."

"We thought nothing of it," Tyson said.

"A few minutes later, the café's lights dimmed, and we looked around and people were ordering dinner." Lana paused. "We were hungry, and the menu looked good, so we said why not?"

"It felt like a date," Tyson said.

∞

When they arrived at Sam's *officetel*, he delicately set Mimi on the couch and covered her in a faux mink blanket. He gave Lana and Tyson his bed and rolled out a yoga mat for himself. Good enough for sit-ups, good enough for sleep, he figured.

"FEMA special delivery," he said as he tossed bottled waters at Lana and Tyson. He left one on the coffee table next to Mimi's purse. Then he turned on the AC, turned off the light, and chugged his bottle of water.

Lying on his back, staring at the ceiling, Sam wondered how Mimi would react in the morning. Would she be nervous or nonchalant? Would she think him a hero or a villain? Would she hang out or sneak out? Would her parents be worried? Had her friend messaged or called?

Sam's ears were still buzzing from the bangers and mashups of Zen. Zen: what a fitting name, he thought. You lose yourself to find yourself. He shut his eyes, took a deep breath, and pictured the stone Buddha bust at the bar's entrance.

∞

Sam sat up and faced the couch. Mimi was now sleeping on her left side, facing the yoga mat. She'd drank the bottled water and set her phone on the coffee table. Lana and Tyson looked comfortable but not overly comfortable. There was no spooning or touching of any sort. Lana slept in the classic fetal position, her left hand resting on her chin. She'd folded her pillow into a double decker. Tyson was on his stomach, his left arm hanging off the side of the bed. He looked like he should've been drooling, but he wasn't.

Sam tiptoed to the bathroom and checked the mirror. He had bed head—or yoga mat head—and puffy eyes. He splashed cold water on his face and patted it down with a hand towel. Then he took a shot of mouthwash and swished it around.

In the kitchen, he poured a glass of water and looked in the fridge. It was nearly empty, save for a red apple and a hangover drink. He popped open the can and raised it in a self-toast.

"For when you break it down 'til the break of dawn."

The lingering mouthwash gave the hangover drink a strange taste, something akin to the mixture of toothpaste and orange juice. He chased it down with the glass of water.

"Rise and shine. Do you wanna order food?" he asked when Lana's head popped up.

"Absolutely. What are our options?"

He checked the time on his phone. "McDonald's breakfast just ended. How about Korean food?"

"Sure. We're in Korea, after all. Can you order? I trust your judgment."

"Me, too," chimed in Tyson.

"Can I eat with you all?" asked Mimi. "I'm famished."

Sam was surprised to see her awake but tried not to show it. "Uh, yeah, sure," he replied. "Anyone want water?"

Lana wanted water and Mimi the bathroom. Sam flipped through the many restaurant fliers that had been taped to his front door that month.

"What happened last night?" Mimi asked when she got out of the bathroom with a fresh coat of makeup and without the Zen stamp on her hand. "Sorry I took your couch."

"No problem. How are you feeling?" asked Sam.

"Like I lost my film."

"Huh?"

"It's a Korean expression. *Pilleumi kkeungyeosseoyo*. My film was cut. I lost my memory. I blacked out."

Sam introduced Mimi to his friends and relayed the night's events. It was Mimi's first time blacking out in a long time, and the last thing she remembered was getting gum out of her purse. Tyson suspected that the gum on his shoe was hers.

"I know where you sleep," he said.

Sam called a restaurant, but no one picked up. When he tried a different number, he got the same result.

"Can you try calling these?" he asked Mimi, holding up the restaurant fliers. "No one's answering. Maybe it's my phone."

She tried her phone with no luck.

"Is it a holiday?" asked Lana.

"Nope. Let's just go to a restaurant," Sam suggested.

"Ahh. I don't wanna get outta bed. Can you bring back food? Pretty please?" Lana half-begged.

"You got it. But it might be a while."

"I'll stay here, too, if that's okay," said Mimi.

"Yup."

Tyson stood up. "All right. The hunters in search of food. Let's do this."

∞

Tyson and Sam stepped outside the building as a stampede of people ran by. There were kids in the street, cars honking.

"I thought Korea was 'The Land of the Morning Calm'?" Tyson quipped.

"Yeah, this isn't normal. I wonder what's up."

They walked to the edge of the sidewalk to scope out the scene. Traffic was at a standstill, runners darted in different directions, and there was a significant police presence. Tyson and Sam tried to make sense of all the commotion, but the sun was in their eyes.

"Maybe we should go back inside?" Tyson asked, rubbing sweat off his forehead. He was really feeling the hangover.

At that moment, a driver rolled down his window and yelled at them in Korean. Tyson and Sam were startled. They didn't understand what he was saying, but body language is all but universal. "Get the hell out of here!" was a fair interpretation. The man pointed at Sam's building, and the friends ran inside. They pressed up against the double pane glass double doors, collecting their thoughts amid a haze of adrenaline.

"What do you think is going on?" Tyson asked between breaths.

"Your guess is as good as mine. Hopefully nothing too crazy."

"That guy in the car seemed plenty worried. Like he thought we were idiots for standing around. Wanna go talk to the girls?" Tyson asked.

"Let's give it a few minutes."

"All right," he said with skepticism. Tyson wasn't sure why Sam wanted to wait and see. But he had an educated guess.

∞

At the dining hall their freshman year, Sam invariably sat facing the front door. He started with the salad bar and selected his seat first.

Tyson favored fewer trips for food, so he took his time and stacked his plate high. His specialty, which he called "Tyson Chicken," was a chicken sandwich on top of chicken Pad Thai.

Sam's salads could be likened to *ikebana*, the Japanese art of flower arrangement. Tyson had made fun of Sam's first salad—romaine greens encircled in a ring of mandarin oranges with Italian dressing and sunflower seeds—so Sam created a new and unique design every day in what became their ongoing joke.

About a month into their friendship, Tyson caught on to Sam's habit of sitting within sight of the front door. So he put it to the test at the dining hall, a sociological study with Sam as the subject. Tyson grabbed fast food, slingshotted around the round tables, and sat at one of the two-seater tables—in the seat he suspected Sam would've taken. When Sam walked up with another magnificent salad, he looked puzzled.

"Why are we sitting here?"

"I'm just switching things up."

Sam gritted his teeth and sat down, his back to the front door. Their conversation that dinner was stale. Sam didn't have much of an appetite.

Tyson thought it was because Sam liked people watching. When Tyson studied at the library, he, too, liked to face the entrance. The influx of eye candy was a welcome distraction from his business books.

As Tyson later learned, Sam had been a lifeguard for three summers. He had a watchful eye and likely had a hero complex. If or when a victim or villain walked through the front door, he was ready to spring into action.

∞

Bloody hands suspended in midair, then arms outstretched and swaying. She of willowy hair and frame slowly entered their field of vision. Feet dragging and legs discolored, a greenish-white. Her body seemed to have a mind of its own, and it was centimetering closer to them.

She hopped, and their hearts jumped. Instinctively, they backed away from the double doors. Was she wounded or warring, a victim or villain, an effect or a cause? She was the embodiment of the fear of ambiguity.

She came to an abrupt stop ten meters from the building. And Tyson had had enough. It was time to get going. He whispered to Sam, and in that instant, her raven hair whipped around her left shoulder, revealing cloudy white eyes, pale sunken cheeks, and bloodstained lips. She raged toward them, dragging her feet and hopping at high speeds.

"… the hell?!" Sam yelled.

They pressed their shoulders up against the double doors, and she slammed into the glass, her palms and forehead bearing the brunt of the impact. Blood streaked down the glass to her battered body laid out on the pavement. Sam and Tyson backed up, their arms bumping. Not missing a beat, she rolled over to her stomach, showed her teeth, and pushed through the doors.

Tyson and Sam weren't down to fight. They didn't understand the enemy. They retreated up the flight of stairs, her hissing and moaning haunting their every step. Fleet-footed double and triple steps. Tyson kicked over a rusty tin can full of cigarette butts and ashes, sending it rattling downstairs.

Room 403, 8-4-3-0. Sam punched in the code while staring back at the stairwell. His hands were shaking. Tyson was on the balls of his feet.

{beep} They burst into the *officetel* and shut the door. Breathing heavily, they stared each other in the eye. Beads of sweat formed on their faces.

Lana walked over. "Are you boys okay?"

Tyson hugged her and held her close. "We should check the news," he said. He searched the room for a TV. There was none.

"Keep the door closed," Sam said.

Lana wondered if they were joking. She was used to their antics, but Tyson had hugged her so sincerely.

Mimi took them at their word. They hadn't taken off their shoes and didn't have food. "What happened?" she asked, concerned.

Sam turned on his computer. "A woman tried to attack us. She has green skin, she's covered in blood, and her eyes are all messed up."

"What do you mean she tried to attack you?" Lana asked in disbelief.

"We can only assume," Tyson explained. "She came after us and ran into the glass door downstairs. Well, she didn't exactly run. She moved like this." He did his best reenactment.

"Are you sure she's not hurt? Maybe she needs help," Mimi questioned.

"No, no, no," Sam replied. "This is no damsel in distress. It's like she's possessed. She was making these noises. Growling. If anything, she needs psychiatric help. I really think she wanted to hurt us."

"We should ring the police," Mimi said.

"We saw a lot of police cars and people running around. Let's check the news," said Sam.

The New York Times, HuffPost, The Guardian, and the BBC didn't bring up any news. Sam checked Naver and read "홍대," "Hongdae" in the headline.

"Mimi, can you translate this?" He stood up and she took over the computer.

"Oh my God," she said with her mouth agape. "'Breaking News: Murders in Hongdae.'" She clicked on the link. "At least nine people are dead, and police are investigating."

"Damn. That sounds about right," Sam said.

"Okay, but how does that explain the woman downstairs?" Tyson asked.

"It doesn't. We can't even begin to explain her."

Mimi picked her phone up off the coffee table. It was 11:37, and the battery was half spent. No messages or missed calls. She rang her mother, and they listened in. Judging by her tone, it was a fairly normal conversation.

"What'd she say?" Sam asked. "I mean, if it's okay for me to ask."

"I told her I was at a friend's home in Hongdae. She hadn't heard the news, and I said I'd stay inside."

"It was that easy?"

"Yeah, she's not a typical Korean mom. She cares, but she gives me a lot of freedom. And this situation is out of character for me."

"Oh, that's good. And your dad?"

"What about him?"

"What's he like?"

"He's a typical Korean dad. Too busy working."

Mimi had referred to Sam as a friend, and he was ever the overthinker. Surely, it was just a white lie she told her mother, right? Technically, they were just friends, if even that. They hadn't so much as kissed. But what if she hadn't blacked out? Or could he have kissed her before then? Or was it better that they hadn't kissed at all? Ah, overthinking! He was never at a loss for thoughts. He'd just met Mimi, and he had more important things to think about than labels and lip-locking.

Sam picked up his phone. "I'll try Steve."

Steve's phone was off, so Sam messaged him a nervous text.

Mimi checked other websites, but there was no new news. The Korean *netizens* were in full force, speculating as to the identities of the murderers. Drunk students? Chinese? Japanese? Americans?

Sam touched his temples. A terrible tension headache had set in. The woman downstairs, Steve, and Mimi were weighing heavy on his mind, but hunger was the likely culprit. And the hangover didn't help. He checked his cupboard. Crunchy peanut butter, whole wheat crackers, a half-full bag of popcorn kernels, and store brand spaghetti. He had a steady supply of tea bags, green for a pick-me-up and chamomile for a knock-me-out.

The crackers were individually wrapped, eight per pack. Opening all seven packs over a white plastic plate, Sam was reminded of childhood 'cracker parties' he and his brothers had had. They'd mix ketchup, mayonnaise, and black pepper in a small glass bowl, put it in the center of a porcelain plate, and surround it with stacks of saltine crackers. These 'cracker parties,' presumably the catalyst of

Sam's dining hall salads, included daytime television programming, trashy talk shows and squeaky clean public broadcasting alike. It was summertime, and the brothers were latchkey kids without cable TV.

Sam ran tap water into two white teacups and two red coffee mugs. For civility's sake, he wished he had a proper teakettle, but the microwave would have to do. Four minutes for four hot waters. He set the cups, mugs, and tea bags on the coffee table so as to avoid more overthinking. Lana and Mimi chose the white teacups, and they all had green tea.

"Not to seem ungrateful, but do you have eggs or meat?" Tyson asked when Sam brought over the peanut butter, crackers, and butter knife.

"Nope."

"First world problems," Mimi remarked.

"Is Korea first world? I haven't seen enough of it to form an opinion." A smirk came over Tyson's face.

Sam came to Mimi's defense. "Don't mind him. He's just trying to ruffle your feathers." He turned his attention to Tyson. "I expect we'll eat out a lot, and we can go grocery shopping together. Don't blame me for the food. Blame the murderers."

"You think it's more than one person?" Lana asked.

"Yeah. I can't imagine just one person doing this, unless they're police or military. Koreans don't have guns. There's no right to bear arms here." He dipped the knife into the jar of peanut butter. "Actually, I know how something like this could happen. At a Korean spa. People have such a false sense of security at *jimjilbang*s." Mimi scrunched her brows. "Think about it," he continued. "When is a person most vulnerable? When they're sleeping. More so in a dark room full of strangers. My friend had his phone stolen in a sleeping room, and it was right next to him. Now what if someone walked into that same room and slashed everyone's throats while they were sleeping?"

Mimi brushed him off. "You Americans have such imagination."

"I'm Korean, too."

∞

Twice or thrice a month, Steve attended a *hweshik*, a company dinner.

ROUND ONE

"When you sex, how many times?" asked his co-worker.

"What's that?" Steve thought he misheard.

"When you sex, how many times, one night?" He stood up and thrust his hips for emphasis.

Steve almost spit out his beer. "Oh, um, I don't know."

"How many times?"

"I… I've never counted."

"Me?" He raised his voice, pounded his chest, and looked Steve straight in the eye. "Seven times!"

"Wow!" Steve feigned amazement at the seven fingers.

"I'm Superman!"

"If you'll excuse me…" Steve got up without waiting for a response. He made his way across the restaurant and found his favorite co-worker.

"Seung-ho, come save me."

"From what?" Seung-ho asked, mid-bite of a beef rib.

"From *whom*. Jang-soon is getting way too personal."

"What's he saying?"

"Too much."

They laughed.

Their bosses called them over. They were sitting in the middle of the table in the middle of the room. Their postures commanded the respect of Joseon dynasty monarchs, and they'd just summoned three pretty young things to their table—office workers two to three years out of high school. One of the bosses spoke to Seung-ho in private.

"They want you to give a toast," Seung-ho reported to Steve. It would be the sixth toast of the night—all extolling the virtues of the company.

"Yeah, okay," Steve agreed, shifting his gaze to the microphone.

"But first they want you to pour shots for everyone."

"Huh?" Steve replied.

"Yeah, they want you to go around to every table."

"Why me?"

"Because you're one of the newest and youngest employees."

Steve closed his eyes and held the bridge of his nose. "In college, I never joined a frat because I didn't wanna be hazed. Here I am working for a Fortune 500 company, and they want me to play bartender."

"What's a frat?" Steve didn't answer. "Listen, this can only help your situation," Seung-ho said. "You shouldn't fight the bosses on this one."

Defiant. In a word, that was Steve's first performance review at work. More a personal than a professional issue, which made it that much worse. Steve's bosses gave him the impression that he was a damaged good, that they could easily replace him with a new employee with a better personality.

Four years earlier, Seung-ho, too, had had a bad first performance review. He'd been habitually late to work and missed some deadlines but had managed to get back in his bosses' good graces. So after Steve's performance review, when Seung-ho saw the deer-in-the-headlights look in the young buck's eyes, he decided to help him.

"I'll do the shots with you," Seung-ho insisted.

"I thought I was pouring shots? Damn it." Steve exhaled. "Hazing for real. I have too much pride for this. But I'm trusting you."

Eleven tables, eleven shots of soju. It was as if their livers were company property.

"Thanks, Seung-ho," Steve said, wrapping his arm around his friend. "You're a heck of a wingman. If you ever need me to take a dozen shots with you…"

"Don't mention it."

They gulped down a few glasses of water before Steve picked up the mic. {tap} {tap}

"If I can have your attention… If I can have your attention, please. I'd like to raise a toast… to the company." He felt like he was swaying. "To a fantastic year." It was July. "Repeat after me. Hip hip hooray! Hip hip hooray!'"

"Hip hip hooray! Hip hip hooray!" They raised their glasses with each cheer.

Steve, usually a skilled toastmaster, felt embarrassed and insecure. He hadn't said 'hip hip hooray' since grade school and had intended to use Korean in his speech. But the language barrier had worked in his favor. His co-workers took his speech in stride.

"Time to move," Seung-ho said.

"Let me guess. A pub?" Steve asked.

"Right."

ROUND TWO

Steve and Seung-ho sat in the corner with a pitcher of beer.

"I never get to play the foreigner card," Steve complained.

"What do you mean?" asked Seung-ho.

"I mean the company doesn't care that I'm American. They treat me just like everyone else. It's ten o'clock and I wanna go home, but I'm expected to stay out and socialize just like you and the other Koreans."

"So the bosses treat you like a standard employee. What's wrong with that? It's fair, isn't it?"

"It's not fair to anyone. We all work overtime. That's the nature of the beast—of working for a *chaebol*. But overtime and then a *hweshik*? This is some bullshit."

"Yeah, bullshit, man!" chimed in Superman, hovering over the table.

Seung-ho and Steve looked at Superman disapprovingly, and he returned to his seat.

Steve continued, "A *hweshik* is more of a burden than a bonus. Sure, we get free food and alcohol, but so what? I'd rather be sleeping, exercising, going on a date… saving my sanity." He poured Seung-ho another beer.

Since joining the company, Steve had developed health problems similar to the side effects of a poorly-tested prescription drug rushed to market: headaches, blurred vision, dizziness, an increase in blood pressure, and tightness in his chest. A dentist said he was teeth grinding and a doctor that he was overbreathing. In both cases, stress was the underlying cause.

"How do you avoid burnout at work?" Steve asked Seung-ho. "I never feel refreshed. Hell, I never feel fresh."

Steve's creativity, the bread and butter of his job as a research and development engineer, was stifled, and his ideas were turning stale.

"I have no secret," Seung-ho replied. "I just try to stay positive. It's either that or quit, right? And I don't think you're a quitter."

"No. No way."

Quitting wasn't an option. Steve had moved to a foreign land, and he was going to succeed, damn it. His plan was to work for the *chaebol* for a few years. Make the big bucks, boost his résumé, toy with the latest technology, and get out with his soul intact. Just short of a deal with the devil and just about the same plan that his San Francisco BigLaw associate friends had.

ROUND THREE

Steve followed his co-workers up the narrow and stuffy stairs, the reverb of a wannabe crooner becoming increasingly audible in their ascent. When they reached the reception room, Steve rolled his eyes. Cheap chandeliers. Checkered tiles. Animal print upholstery. A bow-tied employee. A neon sign that read "Luxury *Noraebang*."

Steve shook a tambourine to the beat of the music. It was the least he could do to keep himself entertained and awake. K-pop wasn't his cup of soda, and K-dramas, which showed behind the lyrics, weren't his scene. Steve's co-workers, perhaps sensing his apathy, egged him on to sing.

"Okay, okay, one song." He reached for the microphone.

He flipped through the fuchsia-colored three-ring binder and fast found a fitting song for the occasion. The Bangles' "Walk Like an Egyptian" to match the room's theme and décor. As Steve sang, he slid his feet on the mosaic floor and shifted and pulled back his arms like a supposed ancient Egyptian. He did his best pole dance on a plastic papyrus column and ran his fingers down the tall statue of King Tut. With his back to the gold hieroglyphic-papered wall, he pressed his hands together and posed for a photo with the bust of Nefertiti. For his grand finale, he dove onto the plush pillow-covered couch.

Steve's co-workers hooted and clapped and called for an encore. He politely declined and broke out into a smile. Maybe, just maybe, he'd had a little bit of fun.

Seung-ho high-fived Steve and excused himself from the room. In his absence, one of the bosses sang love ballads and a male intern an R&B song.

"My wife called. She's mad that I'm not home yet," Seung-ho told Steve.

Steve checked his phone. 2:12 a.m. "Let's go."

They bowed and waved their goodbyes, skipped the *noraebang*'s complimentary ice cream, and found the nearest taxi stand. There was a slight chill in the air.

"Thanks again for looking out for me," Steve said.

A deluxe taxi, black with a yellow sign, pulled up to the curb.

"I know you'd do the same for me," Seung-ho replied.

"Of course."

Their handshake turned into a hug, and Seung-ho hopped in the backseat of the cab.

∞

Shortly before nine the next morning, Seung-ho slashed his wrists with a box cutter in the seventh floor restroom by the conference room.

Steve noticed a shuddering and sobbing intern standing next to two stern police officers.

"What's going on?" Steve asked.

"They'll want to talk to you," the intern mumbled, motioning toward the police officers.

"About what?"

The intern squatted down and continued crying. Steve saw yellow police tape around the restroom.

He approached the receptionist's desk. "Can you tell me what happened?"

She hesitated. "Um…"

He blew past her and knocked on his boss' door.

"*Nay?* Yes?"

"It's me," Steve said, inviting himself in. "Do you know why the police are here? What happened in the restroom?"

His boss took off his reading glasses and laid them on the desk. "No one told you? Lee Seung-ho died."

"No…" Steve covered his face with his hands.

"He cut himself."

"No!" Steve stormed out of the office.

It didn't make any sense. Why would Seung-ho end his own life? He was so full of it. And why would he kill himself at work? He could've done it anywhere, anytime. To commit suicide on company property was like a royal eff you to the Korean royalty that is the *chaebol*.

The police officers and an interpreter found Steve sitting alone in the break room. They expressed their condolences and readied their notepads.

"When was the last time you saw Seung-ho Lee?"

"Last night."

"When exactly?"

"After karaoke. We walked to the taxi stand, and he took the first cab. It was two, maybe two-thirty."

"Do you know why Mr. Lee might have taken his own life?"

"No."

"Did he ever talk about his problems?"

"No. I just told him my problems. He was a good listener." Steve paused. "I thought he was an eternal optimist."

Steve retreated to his cubicle and stared at his all-black screensaver in dismay. In distress. In disbelief. He straightened out a metal paper clip and scratched a line across his left wrist. Seung-ho, his ally. Steve retraced the line with the paper clip. Seung-ho, his fallen comrade. Steve scratched deeper and drew blood. Seung-ho, the friend he barely knew. Steve looked around the office. No one was watching. Shocked by his own actions, he pulled four tissues out of a box and applied pressure to his wound.

∞

Lana brushed her hair, light cinnamon and bra strap length, and looked longingly out the window. A side street view with minimal greenery, a few parked cars, and no pedestrians. Her and Tyson's vacation had just begun, and she had an itinerary. Not with dates and times. He wouldn't go for that. But with places and events, food and housing options. It was an ambitious agenda for their three-week stay—with mini trips to Gyeongju, Busan, and Jeju Island. Then they'd continue on to Japan.

"Do you mind if I open the window?"

"No, not at all," Sam replied.

Lana slid the window open and placed her wooden hairbrush on the sill. She pressed her face against the screen mesh, breathing in the humidity.

Tyson observed her with romantic curiosity. He imagined her eyes closed, a soft smile forming on her lips as she mentally transported herself to a world of bliss.

"Guys…" Mimi started. She was still at the computer. Lana scratched the tip of her nose and turned to face Mimi.

"It's not just Hongdae. It's all of Seoul. I can't... I'm in shock. So many people are dead."

Tyson and Sam rushed over to the computer screen. Accompanying the news article was a map of the city, with a half-dozen locations pinpointed in red.

"How many?" Lana asked. "How many people are dead?"

"At least fifty," Mimi said with a quiver in her voice.

"What's happening?" Lana questioned.

"No one knows yet, or they're not saying."

"What about the police? What do they say?" Lana asked.

"They're telling people to stay home. To lock their doors."

"I think that's for the best," Sam said, "considering the woman downstairs."

Mimi saved some emergency numbers to her phone and Sam reached for his.

"I'll try Steve again," he said.

∞

Away from the lights and sounds of revelry, Steve stumbled through the backstreets of Hongdae, destination unknown. He went up a hill and down another, enveloped in graffitied glass and brick walls. There was a circus scene with a leggy acrobat swinging high above the clouds, and a pastel pink teddy bear and two plate spinners in green uniforms standing atop the big top while a smiling, sinister clown stared from afar. There were music notes. A bucktoothed whale. The all-seeing eye. A tiger with rabbit ears. Snow White with a machine gun, SHAME FOR SALE, and LOVE, PEACE WITH YOU in black stencil. 'Pooing' in simple red lettering. What did the other, illegible tags mean? Only the artists or vandals knew.

A gust of wind blew Steve's button-up up. He tugged his shirttail down and clutched his left arm to his chest, favoring his wrist.

At the end of a quiet street, he sat on the edge of the curb, with litter to his left and a dark alley, home to air conditioning units and public urination, to his right. He'd used the alley before—as a shortcut to a main road. He'd squeezed past the A/C units and climbed ten feet down a utility pole, much to the amusement of passers-by who'd paused and pointed up at him.

Steve rolled up his shirtsleeve and peeled off a bandage to reveal an infected gash. Poking the pink skin, he sucked air through his teeth and spoke with remorse, "Damn." He raised his chin up to the sky, starless. "I should get this looked at. Tomorrow."

Steve started to reapply the bandage when, overtaken by rage, he grabbed and smashed an empty beer bottle. He felt like a gun was being held to his head as he held the bottle's jagged edge to his wrist.

"Ahh!" A swift slice. Blood soaked into Steve's white linen shirt, and tears welled up in his eyes. He thought of Seung-ho and collapsed onto the...

∞

"Any news? Updates?" Tyson asked Mimi. She was mid-text to her friend from Zen.

"No, not really."

"Your family must be worried. Where do you live?" he asked.

"Ilsan."

"Where's that?"

"Northwest of Seoul. About a half-hour away."

"Do you work or study in Seoul?"

"Yes."

"Well, which one?"

Mimi set her phone on the arm of the couch. "I'm a student."

"So you're from Dirty Jerz and commute to the city?"

"Huh?"

"It's like you live in New Jersey and commute to New York City."

She smiled at his attempt to lighten the mood. "I've never been to the U.S., but… maybe? Ilsan is a satellite city on the ring road around Seoul. I think of it like a tree trunk. Seoul is the pith—the center—and the newer satellite cities are the growth rings."

"That's po-e-tic," Tyson syllabled. "Where did you get 'ring road'? I've only heard 'loop' and 'beltway.'"

"I lived in London for two years. A ring road can be as small as a street and as big as a motorway. Anyway, I must be losing my English accent."

"Careful, Mimi," Lana said without a hint of jealousy. "Tyson will stalk you if you tell him too much about yourself."

Mimi opened her mouth wide and pressed her hands to her cheeks, feigning terror.

"So what school do you go to?" Tyson continued in jest.

"An all-women's uni," Mimi said with a suspicious sideways glance.

Sam turned off the gas burner and slipped on a floral print oven mitt. With a stained kitchen towel in his left hand, he poured the neon orange pot over a white plastic colander, shielding his face from the steam. He shook and bounced the spaghetti before reintroducing it to the pot.

"Anyone hungry?" Sam asked. He divided the spaghetti onto four plates and offered up extra virgin olive oil and black pepper. "I don't have spaghetti sauce."

"Where do you keep your forks?" Tyson asked.

"In the cabinet above the sink. Can you get four glasses, too?"

"You got it."

Lana set the water filter pitcher on the table. Mimi liberally poured olive oil and conservatively sprinkled pepper onto her plate, then pushed them Lana's way.

"Do you like cooking?" Lana asked Sam.

"Not really. I eat out a lot."

Mimi was meditatively breaking up a brain-shaped clump of spaghetti with her fork.

"So, Mimi, what are you thinking?" Sam asked. "You're not gonna brave the storm and go home, are you? You're welcome to stay here as long as you need to."

"Thank you. I appreciate that. I'll go home as soon as it's safe, of course."

"Yeah, we'd better wait for word from the police. It shouldn't be long now," Lana said to Mimi. "Besides, I like having you around."

Mimi wasn't sure how to interpret that. Did Lana enjoy her company or her translation skills?

Dessert was the lone red apple, cut into eight slices and rust-tinged from oxidation.

∞

They say that love is eternal. But what about hate? What happens to hatred when the hater dies? Does it disappear? Can it reappear? Is the hated exonerated?

They say that time heals all wounds.

{gasp} Seung-ho snapped his jaws in the air and exhaled a cloud of mist. His body in an advanced state of rigor mortis, he stiffly scratched at the stainless steel walls of the morgue's temperature-controlled room, a glorified freezer.

∞

Steve peeled his purpling face off the concrete, its dirt and pebbles embedded into his cheek and forehead. His body in the early stages of rigor mortis, he cracked his bones and muscles as he got up onto his knees.

∞

The clanging and banging of Seung-ho's freezer got the attention of a crematory technician. The tech slid out Seung-ho's tray and was sure that he was witnessing a miracle, a mythical man come-back-to-life. Frostbitten but alive. He leaned in to try to make sense of Seung-ho's moaning and got fanged in the face.

∞

A stumbling and mumbling late-night reveler, a peace-loving Canadian expat, squinted his eyes at Steve and asked, "Hey, man, are you all right?" Steve's reply was an attack to the throat. The hard partier hit the ground hard, spilling crimson onto the curb.

∞

Do morticians and crematory technicians ever envision how their own bodies will be treated after death? {thud} Seung-ho dropped the crematory technician's corpse on the cold linoleum floor, sans ceremony.

∞

Steve's mouth runneth over with blood. What does blood with an alcohol content of 0.15% taste like to the undead? Sweet and strong. Steve let it linger in his mouth a little, like he would with whiskey.

∞

Bodies rose from the earth and flew down from the sky—from death to life, from life to death. The circle of life. Corpses clawed their way out of coffins and burial mounds, splinters and soil stuck under their fingernails. People plummeted from high-rises onto the streets and sidewalks of Seoul.

Lana, Tyson, and Sam huddled behind Mimi, in front of the computer, as she shakily relayed the news: The president of Korea had declared a state of emergency. An estimated two hundred Seoulites were dead—victims of murder and possible suicides. Police and witnesses described the murders as gruesome and personal, with victims' faces smashed and mashed. Police officers accounted for a dozen of these murders, and in retaliation, police had killed eight alleged murderers. The alleged murderers matched the description of the woman downstairs: less than human.

"And…" Mimi gulped. "Cemeteries in Seoul are reporting that corpses are rising from—"

"Stop!" Lana yelled, taking a step back from the group, her hands in surrender position. "That's enough." She scanned their faces. "You two say you saw some monster woman downstairs. And you—Now you're telling me that zombies are real, and they're attacking Seoul?"

"I don't know what they are," Mimi replied. "Please don't kill the messenger. I'm scared, too."

Lana got misty-eyed and stared straight at Tyson—a piercing gaze.

He spoke calmly and tenderly, "Lana, I wouldn't make this up. We wouldn't make this up." Sam pursed his lips and nodded.

"Then what the hell is going on?" Lana asked, wiping her tears away with her fingers.

Sam clicked over to HuffPost, and there it was, the headline story.

CHAOS IN KOREA

The news mirrored Mimi's, with an addition and a subtraction. U.S. forces in Korea were ready to intervene, and no mention was made of reanimated corpses. HuffPost users suspected that North Koreans or bath salts were to blame for the grisly murders. One user combined the theories: "the north koreans have weaponized bath salts. the zombie apocalypse is here!!!!"

∞

{blam} Law and disorder at the morgue. Tattered uniforms. Scattered badges. Shattered limbs. Shrapnel-shredded skin. {cough} {cough} {cough} Dust-filled lungs. Eyes that stung. Shell shock. Cremation urns had exploded like gunpowder, and Seung-ho swept through the ash clouds, dismembering members of the police squad.

∞

Three siren-less squad cars surrounded Steve. "Stay there!" a female officer shouted. She'd seen the Canadian sprawled out on the street a few blocks back, surrounded by curious and concerned early birds and all-nighters. Steve hobbled toward the officer, looking like he'd just brawled in every bar in Hongdae—the leader of a pub crawl fight club. "Stop! Now!" she yelled in English.

∞

When the dust settled, a hodge-podge of headless and limbless bodies, ripped and bloodied beige and blue uniforms, porcelain pieces, and Seung-ho remained contained in the room of the morgue. The funeral director had heard the blasts of the exploding urns and the dying screams of the police officers, and armed himself with a fire iron—a glorified fireplace poker—from the crematory. He tiptoed into the now-quiet room, and Seung-ho charged, his back and claws arched. The funeral director sidestepped the raging bull and stabbed him in the back. Seung-ho stopped, staggered, and fell to his side, the fire iron jutting out from his chest. To the funeral director, the incident was a blur. And to Seung-ho, reanimation and re-death were less than a blur.

∞

Steve didn't get within a bull's roar of the female officer. The three male officers beat him back with batons, then beat him down. And Steve had no mind to block himself from the brutality. He attacked, rolling back onto his feet and, off-balance, lunging at a male officer. Claws connected with hips, and Steve and the cop crashed onto the pavement. Immediately, the second policeman yanked Steve back by the collar, and the third battered away at Steve's rib cage—a makeshift batting cage. Steve was hunched over on the median of the road, gasping for air, when the female officer stepped to his side and cracked his ribs with her baton. She left him breathless.

II

{flash}{boom} The sky took a candid group photo through the *officetel* window. Mimi was frantically pacing the room, on the phone with her parents. Lana, Sam, and Tyson were on the couch, fidgeting, trying to talk their way through the situation.

{flash}{boom} The lightning and thunder only added to the terror. The news had confirmed that the dead were coming back to life.

Mimi hung up the phone, her mouth still half open. Her arms hung to her sides as she stood staring at the swirls and lines of the wooden floor.

"I can't go back to Ilsan," she said a minute later. "My parents can't drive down to get me."

"So you'll stay with us," Sam said, nodding his head.

"Yeah. Thanks," she replied, looking down, biting her lip.

"What will your family do?" Lana asked.

"They're going to the Costco in our neighborhood."

"To stock up on supplies?" Tyson asked.

"To stay. It's basically a bomb shelter."

"It has everything you could want or need…" Lana said.

"And it's deep underground," Mimi added.

"That's a solid plan. I'm sure your family will be safe there," Tyson said.

"Thank you. I certainly hope so."

"Is there a Costco around here?" Lana asked Sam.

"Not in Hongdae."

"So what are we gonna do?" Tyson asked. "We have no food."

"We'll figure it out," Sam replied. "Let's call home first."

Sam, Lana, and Tyson took turns video calling their families. They shed tears, exchanged I-love-yous, and promised to keep their loved ones updated.

"You two please protect her," Lana's mother pleaded with Tyson and Sam. Lana still lived at home—like Mimi.

Mimi rested her elbows on the windowsill, worried about her family's fate. Her mother. Her little brother. Her father. Would they make it to Costco without incident? Would their Gold Star Membership card grant them entry? Would they be safe there? Could she find a way to get to them?

Raindrops rolled down the window, and Mimi thought about the game she and her brother often played. Raindrop racing. They'd each pick a raindrop and see whose reached the finish line—the bottom of the windowpane—first. It was a simple game with a complex concept: The whole is greater than the sum of its parts. As a raindrop raced down the window, it would stick to other raindrops and grow bigger. Cohesion. And as the raindrop grew bigger, it became greater—faster.

With her family, Mimi knew what to expect. They had a real relationship built on love, trust, and respect. They had synergy. Raindrops.

But Mimi didn't know what to expect from Sam, Lana, and Tyson. Their relationship was superficial, built on alcohol. And there was no time for her to test the waters. She'd have to stick with them, and they'd have to form a bond—fast.

∞

Officials warned residents of Seoul not to use tap water for drinking, cooking, washing, or bathing.

"That leaves us with two bottles and a half-pitcher of water," Sam announced. Judging by his tone of voice, the pitcher was half-empty.

"Okay, so now what?" Tyson revived the discussion. "We need a plan."

"I say we wait it out," Sam said.

Tyson raised his brows. "You wanna stay here, holed up, with just water and popcorn?"

"No, of course that's not what I want. But it's our best option for now."

"I say we get outta Seoul ASAP," Tyson said.

"And go where? Korea is a densely-populated peninsula. These vampires, or whatever the hell they are, will be all over the country in no time."

"Exactly. Let's get going while we still can."

"Tyson, you saw the woman downstairs. Imagine her multiplied times a hundred, a thousand. How are we gonna get past that?"

"By actually trying," Tyson said.

"It's not that simple," Sam said, his voice deeper than usual. "Why force the issue?"

"Guys," Mimi intervened between the warrior and the worrier, "what's our immediate concern?"

"Food and water," Lana answered.

"Right. And Sam, you have neighbors. Neighbors share."

"I don't know my neighbors."

"That's okay," Mimi insisted. "Most Koreans don't know their neighbors either."

"Again, I *am* Korean. I was born here," Sam said, narrowing his eyes.

"I didn't mean it like that," Mimi replied, taken aback.

"Then what did you mean?" he asked.

"Sam, can we not do this? I know you're Korean and American."

"So let's meet the neighbors in the morning?" Lana intervened this time.

They said "yes" in unison.

∞

{ding} {dong} {ding} {dong} Mimi and Lana stood smiling and waving in front of the peephole camera. Tyson and Sam stood by their sides, knives to their sides, out of the camera's view. Ten, twenty seconds. There wasn't so much as a peep.

They moved on to the next door. {ding} {dong} {ding} A middle-aged man hurried them into the *officetel*.

"What are you doing out there?" the man scolded Mimi in Korean. "Don't you follow the news?"

"Yes. We're looking for help," she spoke diplomatically.

"What kind of help?"

"Food for starters."

"Are you planning to rob me for it?" he asked.

"What do you mean?" she replied with furrowed brows.

"There's a knife out in the hallway."

Mimi looked back at Sam and Tyson. "They brought knives for protection. They almost got attacked yesterday."

"How? Where?"

"A woman chased them into this building. They say she looked and acted crazy."

"So where's the other knife?"

"Do either of you have a knife on you?" Mimi asked Tyson and Sam.

Sam put his hand up. "I do." He pulled a steak knife out of his back pocket and slowly set it on the floor, as though he were in a hostage situation.

"How do you know these foreigners? Are they your friends?" the man asked.

"Yes, we're friends, and he lives on your floor." Mimi pointed at Sam, who bowed until his eyes met his second-to-top button.

"We don't want any trouble," Sam spoke up. "We're here because I don't have food in my *officetel*, and we don't feel safe going outside." Mimi translated.

"Very well." The neighbor relaxed. "I'll feed you all."

Spam, tuna, and Vienna sausage cans covered the oak wood dining table, and an assortment of assorted nuts, snacks, and ramen topped the marbleized kitchen countertop. Lonely guy food. Liters of water lined the white baseboards.

"Where'd he get all this food and water?" Lana asked.

"He was in his taxi when he heard the news. So he drove to the nearest grocery store and bought them out," Mimi translated.

"Before the panicked people," Lana said.

"Precisely."

Mr. Shin, the neighbor and host, sliced Spam, Vienna sausages, and tofu. Sam peeled onions and potatoes and Lana chopped them up, along with a healthy head of cabbage and kimchi.

"Kimchi looks like rotting human flesh," Lana remarked.

"Wow," Sam said with laughter. "Way to insult an entire nation."

"This is the first time I've heard that," Mimi said to Lana.

"Look at it up close. The pale white and yellowish tint—it's skin. And the red—that's blood," Lana explained.

"I see what you mean." Mimi nodded. "But I wish you hadn't said that."

"I hope I'm not being rude. It's just an observation."

"Oh, no, I'm not being nationalistic. It's not like I have a patriotic palate. But we're about to eat. And I have a weak stomach."

Their stomachs rumbled as the smell of the hodgepodge stew, with the inclusion of ramen (and the exclusion of its seasoning packet) and *gochujang*, filled the air.

Mimi and Tyson cleared the dining table and arranged the place settings: flat, stainless steel chopsticks, long spoons, chipped sky blue ceramic bowls, and dark green plastic tumblers.

With steam hitting his face, Mr. Shin placed the bubbling pot in the middle of the table. He ladled the stew into his bowl, getting just the right proportion of portions. He favored Spam. Then it was every man and woman for themselves. Mimi filled everyone's water cups while they filled their bowls.

"What do you call this?" asked Tyson, scooping the stew out of his bowl.

"*Budae jiggae*," Mimi answered. "Army base stew."

"Was it made by the military?" Lana asked.

"By Koreans during the war. We didn't have much food, so we used leftover ingredients from U.S. Army bases and got creative."

"Ah, so that explains the Spam and Vienna sausages," Tyson said. "I didn't expect this to be so good. My compliments to the chef."

Mr. Shin brushed him off. "This is easy to make and tastes even better with American cheese," Mimi translated.

Mr. Shin offered up soju, and they all politely declined.

"Silly me," Mr. Shin feigned embarrassment. "We're practically at war."

"Interesting choice of words," Sam observed. "Why is he comparing our situation to war?"

"Well," Mimi said after a long chat with Mr. Shin, "he has a theory."

∞

According to Chinese belief, people have a yang and yin of souls: rational and irrational. Upon physical death, the rational soul ascends on high. But the irrational soul remains intact and dormant. And if someone lived a bad life, died a bad death, or becomes unsettled or upset in death, the irrational soul can reanimate the body, creating a *jiangshi*, a "stiff corpse." A monster that hops.

"*Jiangshi*? Really?" Lana grumbled.

"Well, it's pronounced *gangshi* in Korean," Mimi clarified.

"Thanks for the language lesson, but I don't—"

"Hey, hey," said Tyson, leaning into Lana. She closed her eyes (rather than roll them in disbelief) and took a deep breath, her abdomen rising and falling.

55

"Let's suppose Mr. Shin is right," Sam said. "Why are *gangshi* here in our city... in our neighborhood... in our building?"

"Like he said, maybe they died badly. They were violently killed. Murdered. Wrongfully executed. Prematurely buried. Suicides," Mimi translated.

"But people die horrible deaths everywhere, every day," said Lana. "And they don't collectively come back from the dead. So why would this happen here and now?"

Mimi consulted Mr. Shin, froze up, then consulted her phone. Lana took a sip of warm water.

"I had to look up a word," Mimi said. "Shaman. Witch doctor. Necromancer. Mr. Shin thinks someone might be controlling the corpses."

"Imagine that," Lana said with a hollow laugh. "Someone raised an army of the undead."

"Is it possible to track down a necromancer?" Sam asked.

"Not that he knows of," said Mimi.

"I'm sorry," Lana said, "but this is a lot to digest. Can you please thank Mr. Shin for the meal and ask if we can come back tomorrow?"

"Of course," Mimi spoke for Mr. Shin. He shook open a yellow plastic Mapo District garbage bag and filled it with tuna, ramen, chips, nuts, and water.

Sam accepted the bag with both hands and thanked Mr. Shin. "*Kamsahamnida.*"

"I'll stay back and do the dishes," Mimi told the group.

"I'll help," said Sam, handing the bag off to Tyson.

"Thank you. We'll wash them next time," Lana said.

"What's your passcode?" Tyson asked Sam.

"Eight-four-three-zero."

"Can I borrow your knife for a second?"

Tyson stepped out into the hallway, ready to fend off an attack, and picked his own knife up off the tile floor. Lana returned Sam's steak knife and nodded goodbye to Mr. Shin.

Sam put his hand on Mimi's arm, just below her shoulder. "Thank you for translating for us, in spite of our skepticism."

"No, I get it. It's all right. I'm just as lost as you are." She flipped on the faucet and waited for the water to warm up.

∞

Lana and Tyson plunked down on the couch. He wrapped his arm around her shoulders and held her close.

"I'm not used to this side of you," he said.

"Elaborate," she said with an upward inflection. "Are you talking about my right profile or my personality?"

"Remember when you took Intro to Religion?"

"Yeah?"

"And you studied everything from the Amish to… what was the Z religion?"

"Zoroastrianism," she replied.

"Right. And—"

"You got the idea for your class—to write a business proposal for an Amish taxi service." Lana laughed with crinkly eyes and nose.

"Hey! I got an A on that project," he bragged. "My professor said it was literally ahead of its time."

"But that it wouldn't work."

"I bet it would work now."

"Oh? How so?" she asked.

"As a ridesharing service."

"What would you do—make a ridesharing app for the Amish? For them to use on phones they don't have?"

"A lot of the new generation has phones."

"I stand corrected. And I apologize to the Amish."

"Consider the potential. Ridesharing is now worth more than the entire taxi industry. And there are a few hundred thousand Amish. How many Zorro… ass… tree… inns," he mumbled, "are there?"

"I have no idea. But you should apologize to them for mispronouncing their name."

"I apologize to the Z people," Tyson said with sincerity. He pulled her in and kissed her, half on the lips, half on the cheek.

"So when you took Religion 101, you said you went to class with an open mind."

"I did. I wanted to suspend disbelief... rule out all possibilities," Lana explained.

"Do you think you can do that again?"

"With what? Mr. Shin's theory?"

"Yeah," Tyson replied.

"Look in my eyes." Lana paused. "I'm scared. And it's not fair to compare this to a college course. This is real life. There are dead people running around out there, and I'm having a hard enough time wrapping my head around that. The idea of *gangshi*... of a necromancer... that's even more unbelievable."

{beep} Sam and Mimi stepped into the *officetel* and kicked off their shoes.

"We're invited for breakfast tomorrow," Sam said.

Tyson and Lana offered no response.

"Thanks again for washing the dishes," Lana said some seconds later.

"It was no trouble at all," Mimi replied. "There's a strange comfort in doing the dishes."

"Yeah, I know what you mean." Lana nodded. "Water has a calming effect."

"Mimi," Sam spoke from across the room, "can you check your phone?"

"What for?"

"Mine has no signal."

Hers didn't either. She scrolled through the phone's settings. "Let's try restarting them?"

Still no service. Sam fired up the computer and tapped his nails on the table.

"Phew!" he exhaled after the startup sound.

"Do we have internet?" asked Tyson.

"Yeah." Sam hunched over and clicked over to HuffPost. Lana came up behind him and looked over his shoulders.

"What's the word?" Tyson asked.

"It's a slaughter out there," Sam reported.

"Please spare us the details," Mimi said.

Hongdae was ground zero for the *gangshi* invasion. Outside the university's main gate, an art major and her masterpiece lay in pieces. At a cutesy coffee shop, a couple in matching outfits was torn to shreds. The playground became a battleground, littered with bottles and bodies. Hostels became hostile. On a Sangsu sidewalk, a stroller was tipped over and caked in blood. A closer look revealed a dead teacup dog inside. At a Hapjeong *gimbap* shop, a ramen-haired grandmother left her last meal untouched. A zombie-like gamer exited a *PC bang*. Instakilled.

"We're being evacuated," Sam said.

"Who is *we*?" asked Mimi.

"Americans," he replied with a gulp.

"I thought so," she spoke slowly, solemnly.

"Families of the U.S. military and government employees are being ordered to evacuate."

"What about us?" asked Tyson.

"We're *authorized* to evacuate."

"Where's the evacuation point?" Lana asked.

"Mokdong Ice Rink or Jamsil Sports Complex. We're closer to the ice rink."

"Do you know how to get there?" Tyson asked.

"Yeah, but–"

"Let's get going," Tyson cut him off.

"How?" Sam questioned. "There's no public transportation."

"And taxis aren't running," Lana added.

"People are recommending that we fly commercial because there's no guarantee of evacuation. Of course, that's assuming we can book a flight and get to the airport. And we've already been over this. It's not safe outside."

"So you still wanna wait it out?" Tyson asked Sam.

"Yes, that hasn't changed."

"You're psyching yourself out," Tyson said. "Why stay stuck to the computer screen? Waiting might mean dying."

"Then what do you propose?" Sam asked.

"Well, there's a taxi driver next door."

"He's a man who happens to be a taxi driver," Sam said. "I'm a teacher, but I'm sure as hell not teaching today."

"Guys, what about Mimi?" asked Lana.

"You don't have to protect me," Mimi said. "I can take care of myself."

"I'm sure you can," Tyson said. "But we'll find a way to get you outta here. If not outta Korea, then at least outta Seoul."

∞

Mimi and Tyson stood side by side. {ding} {dong} {ding}

"Sorry to bother you, Mr. Shin…"

"It's no bother," he said. "What do you need?"

"Well, I'm sure you've heard that the Americans are evacuating."

"Yes, I follow the news."

Mimi nodded. "My friend wants to know if you'd consider driving us to Mokdong Ice Rink or one of the airports."

Mr. Shin stared at Tyson. "Tell your friend he's crazy. It's absolute hell out there."

"You're crazy," she deadpanned to Tyson. He looked away, half-embarrassed, half-disappointed.

Mr. Shin bit his lip in thought. "I'll tell you what, though. You and your friends do some research on *gangshi*. Then, if you still want to make a run for it, we'll talk."

"Thank you," Mimi said. "We'll see you in the morning."

"Okay. Eight o'clock."

∞

Mr. Shin cracked in the fifth and final egg and covered the skillet until the whites set. Tyson put spoons on the table and water in the plastic tumblers. Mimi scooped the kimchi fried rice into the ceramic bowls.

"The bowls, please," Mr. Shin said with his right hand out. He slipped a spatula under the eggs and set one on each bed of rice. The garnish was dried and seasoned seaweed.

"You're forcing my hand," Mr. Shin said when they sat down. "I didn't expect you all to show up with bags."

Three bags of essentials: food, water, clothes, towels, a flashlight, toilet paper, garbage bags, ibuprofen, bandages, credit cards, cash in two currencies, passports, weapons, phones, and chargers.

"The internet was down when we woke up," Mimi said. "And we all agreed it was time to go."

"Your generation," Mr. Shin said with a grumble. "You can't live without technology."

"Well, we don't know what's going on out there or whom to trust. What if the government shut down the internet?" Mimi asked.

"What weapons did you bring?" Mr. Shin asked in return.

Knives, scissors, lighters, forks, and chopsticks.

"Didn't you research *gangshi*?"

"Yes," Mimi replied, "but assuming that we're dealing with *gangshi*, some of the information we found seems… inaccurate."

"Like what?"

"We read that *gangshi* don't do well in the sun—that the heat can burn them to ashes. But it was midday when the woman downstairs chased Tyson and Sam."

"Okay. What else do you think is inaccurate?" asked Mr. Shin.

"The woman downstairs didn't dress the part. Traditionally, *gangshi* wear Qing dynasty clothing," Mimi replied.

"Do ghosts dress in white sheets?" Mr. Shin asked rhetorically.

"It's like Mr. Shin is speaking in riddles," Mimi said to the group. "He just keeps asking questions. Who has the list?"

Tyson rested his spoon in his bowl. He'd broken his fast, as had Lana and Sam. Mimi and Mr. Shin had only swallowed their words. Tyson reached into his right pocket and handed Mimi a pink note. In his chicken scratch handwriting was a list of *gangshi* weaknesses: sunlight, fire, mirrors, the blood of a chicken or black dog, rice, garlic, salt, vinegar, urine, running water, their blindness, and placing a yellow talisman on one's forehead.

"Right," Mr. Shin agreed. "Rice is a weakness because *gangshi* suffer from arithmomania, a compulsion to count. They have to stop and count each and every grain of rice. But their blindness isn't necessarily a weakness. They make up for it with a heightened sense of smell. That's how they find you. They smell your breath."

"So what if we hold our breath?" Tyson asked.

"Then you get away."

"Don't the rice and mirrors and blindness contradict each other? I mean, if they were blind, how would they know that there's rice to count? And why would mirrors bother a blind... person?" Lana asked.

"I see your point, but I don't have all the answers," Mimi translated for Mr. Shin.

"Still, how does he know so much about *gangshi*?" asked Sam.

"Childhood books and movies."

"In these childhood books and movies, how did people kill *gangshi*?" Lana asked.

"Like this," Mimi said, holding up the pink note.

"Is there a cure for *gangshi*?" Sam asked.

"No, because this is supernatural—not science," Mimi translated, in spite of her scientific studies. "It's not a virus."

"So what's it gonna take for Mr. Shin to drive us to the airport or ice rink?" Tyson asked. "Do I need to piss in a pot or sacrifice a chicken?" Mimi only translated his first question.

"He won't take us," Mimi said, shaking her head, "to either place." Lana, Sam, and Tyson stared at one another, wide eyed. "He'll try to get us to the U.S. Embassy."

"Wait, what?" Lana asked, half relieved. "Why the embassy?"

"For one, the airports are too far away," Mimi replied.

"Okay," Tyson spoke with understanding. "And the ice rink?"

"The U.S. evacuation plan has been on the internet for years. Someone writes an article about it every time North Korea threatens to attack us. And it was all over the news yesterday. So Mr. Shin is convinced that the ice rink will be overrun by Koreans and other non-Americans. Call it a gut feeling."

Gangshi felt the guts of their victims, warm to the touch. Mokdong Ice Rink was a mucky mess, knee deep in body parts of Americans who'd expected to be evacuated and Koreans and other foreign nationals who'd hoped against hope for evacuation. Tens of thousands of broken limbs and dreams. Plans on ice.

"So why would Mr. Shin drive us to the U.S. Embassy?" asked Sam.

"He thinks it's your best chance for evacuation. And the embassy is in Gwanghwamun, so we wouldn't have to cross the river. No doubt the bridges are backed up by now," Mimi explained.

A mass exodus ended with an early exit for thousands of Seoulites. Bridges south, including the neighboring Seongsan, Yanghwa, Seogang, and Mapo, became bridges to the afterlife. Cars crashed. Trucks crushed. Motorcycles flipped. Ambulances stalled. Jaws of death ripped away at vehicles and passengers. People plunged into the Han River in despair. The city was cut in half.

Mimi and Lana tied their shoelaces. The latter had had an extra pair of lattice-laced running shoes and ankle socks.

"Sharing is caring," Lana said.

Tyson heaved up the heaviest of the three bags, a black canvas backpack. Sam handed Mr. Shin a note with his *officetel* passcode.

"Mr. Shin is welcome to take anything he wants," he told Mimi.

"You don't owe me anything," Mr. Shin said through Mimi.

"It's not as noble as it seems," Sam explained. "My employer pays for my housing. And they furnish it." He flashed a smile.

Beyond his dining area, Mr. Shin's *officetel* was bare bones. No bed, no couch, no art. Yet the divorced taxi driver had let them into his humble home and life.

"Thank you," Mr. Shin said. "I'll drive you as far as I can." He and Sam picked up the two other bags, leather messenger and teal drawstring.

"Ready?" Tyson asked the group. He held the door handle. His knife was in his left hand.

"Remember," Mr. Shin said, "*gangshi* aren't human. They may look or act like us, but they're predators. They just want to feed on your energy."

"What energy?" asked Sam.

"Your *qi*. Your life force," Mr. Shin answered. "Protect yourselves. *Gangshi* are mindless killers, senseless slaves."

"The necromancer is their master," Lana thought aloud.

"Yes," said Mr. Shin. "There are powerful, evil people in this world, and we lose sight of that." Mimi finished translating, Mr. Shin looked at the door, and Tyson opened it.

∞

Tyson shut and locked the door. He, Lana, and Sam squeezed the bags between their legs. Lana rode bitch. Mimi rode shotgun. Mr. Shin gunned the engine and made a sharp right turn out of the parking garage, his orange taxi the only vehicle visible on Yanghwa Road. He went well past the speed limit, past high-rise after high-rise.

Lana caught a glimpse of graffiti on a storefront. A winged silhouette. Was it a guardian angel or an angel of death? A savior or a slayer? Were its wings divine or dark? Would it deliver or destroy humanity?

Lana had contemplated angels ever since she was one herself. Growing up in a three-generation Cuban-American household, she'd received a double dose of Catholicism. Bible study on school days and Sundays. Rigid nuns and nannies. Devout grandparents and parents. A heavenly and earthly father. She'd been daddy's little angel.

Mr. Shin angled onto Sinchon Road, weaving in and out of the way of wrecked and abandoned autos. He sped through traffic lights and CCTV cameras, none of which were working. When he made it to the top of the hill, Mr. Shin cursed and slammed his palms on the steering wheel. They all saw what he saw. A car graveyard with *gangshi* creeping around. It was like Judgment Day. Glass, metal, and plastic appeared to have fallen from the sky. *Gangshi* were hunched over, gagging and vomiting.

Mr. Shin crossed the median and continued driving in the wrong direction—past department stores and just past Sinchon Station. But both sides of the street were blocked up. A dead end. The taxi came to a sudden stop.

"You'll have to take it from here, or I'll take you all back with me," Mr. Shin said in a rush.

"We've gotta go," Mimi translated to the backseat.

Mr. Shin pursed his lips and took one last look at them. "*Jal ka.*" Go well. Take care.

The left rear door of the taxi was locked, so they got out on the right side. Mr. Shin rolled down his window and scattered a pocketful of rice across the concrete. The friends didn't see it, and the *gangshi* ignored it.

Mr. Shin hit reverse and floored it, and the *Haechi* logo on the rear door became a blur. *Haechi*, *Haetae*, the mythical unicorn lion. The symbol of Seoul. The protector of Korea.

"Over there," Sam said, thinking on his feet.

They sprinted and dropped their bags and weapons on the front steps of the police station. {tap} {tap} {tap} Sam looked through the glass. {tap} {tap} {tap} They all cupped their palms to the glass and leaned forward, their brown eyes scanning the room. Empty desks and coffee mugs. Bureaucratic forms waiting to be filled out—in pen. Pens adorned with the Korean National Police University's eagle logo. Stellar's sea eagle, *Haliaeetus pelagicus*, a species that winters in South Korea. But where were its watchful eyes and protective wings in the dead of summer?

Sam pulled out his knife. "Let's go," he said. He knew Sinchon well enough, having spent many a Friday night there with Steve.

"Hurry!" he yelled back to Mimi, Lana, and Tyson.

"Where are we going?" Tyson asked, scanning the area for signs of life or death.

"A motel."

They ran uphill through the semi-seedy love motel district. Split in two pairs—Mimi and Sam, Lana and Tyson—they tried their luck knocking on doors. Knock, knock, ginger. Ding dong ditch.

"Hey!" a lady called out from an open glass door. Mimi hid her scissors and followed the lady's voice. Sam stayed in the sun, ready to flag down Lana and Tyson if the lady let them inside.

∞

Room 315

Features and amenities: Black and white swirl wallpaper. White bedding with red heart-shaped pillows. Candy apple red faux leather couch. PC. Wall-mounted TV. Coffee machine. Mirrored walls and ceiling.

Lana swung the drawstring bag on the couch and looked over at Tyson. "They're so damn scary," she said with a shaky voice.

"Hey now." Tyson stepped toward her. "We're safe." He pulled her in for a hug.

"Yeah, for now. But what about the next time?" She paused and exhaled. "How could anyone ever be ready for this? These green... things. They're worse than anything I've ever seen or imagined."

∞

Room 317

Features and amenities: Hot pink walls decorated with a montage of lingerie models. Cherry blossom pink bedding. Black faux leather couch. Black two-seater table and chairs. Wall-mounted TV...

Mimi turned it on. A blank screen.

Sam wiped the sweat off his brow and turned on the A/C. "Are you okay with sharing a bed?" he asked Mimi.

"That's why we're here, right?" she asked.

"Wha-what?"

"I'm kidding," she said with a grin. "It's fine."

"We're gonna owe so many people so much," Sam said, changing the subject. "Mr. Shin. Mrs. Jang..."

"Yeah."

Room 315

Tyson sprawled out on the queen size bed, holding a heart-shaped pillow in each hand. Lana nudged in and laid her head on his chest, her hair tickling his neck and chin. He wrapped his arms around her torso and placed the velvety hearts over her eyes. Her cheeks dimpled. Their bodies formed an acute angle.

They stared at their reflections in the mirrored ceiling. He in a white v-neck, chambray shorts, and gray ankle socks. His face stubbled and hair unruly. She in a light gray off shoulder t-shirt, denim shorts, and white no show socks. Her face make-up free and hair still smooth. They held hands as if they were on a sinking ship. And they sank into a slumber…

∞

{knock} {knock} {knock}

"Hey, we gotta plan," Sam said. Mimi had a bag of food.

Tyson ran his hand through his hair and nodded with closed eyes. "Always. Perpetual planning."

"Wake up, Sleeping Beauty," Sam spoke with no sweetness.

"I'm up, I'm up." Lana rolled out of bed and washed her face with cool water. Tyson took a peek in the bag of food.

"We're racing the clock," Mimi said. "What if we get to the embassy and it's closed?"

"Yeah, we gotta go soon," said Sam.

"But what if *gangshi* grow stronger when the sun goes down?" Lana asked with a yawn. "Let's leave at the crack of dawn."

They agreed.

"So how are we getting to the embassy?" Sam asked. "Cars are out of the question."

"How about bikes?" Lana asked.

"Now there's a thought," Sam replied. "I know someone who biked from Seoul to Busan. We could do the same."

"*You* could do the same," Mimi said. "I can't bike three hundred kilometers."

"This is fight or flight, isn't it? I'm sure you could fly if you had to," Sam said.

She shook her head no.

"Traveling south makes a lot of sense," Tyson said. "There will be far fewer *gangshi* between here and Busan. And we could use the compasses on your smartphones. GPS should still work, even without service."

"Yes, we can still use the GPS satellites. But like I said before, the southbound bridges are probably backed up by now," Mimi said.

"And we don't have bikes just yet. Did anyone see any on the way here?" Lana asked.

"At the subway station," Mimi said. "Locked to the bike racks."

"Yes!" Sam said with unexpected excitement. A eureka moment. He pointed at Lana. "Bikes." Then he shifted his attention to Mimi. "On the subway."

"Are you suggesting that we take bikes on the tracks?" Tyson asked.

"Bingo," Sam said.

"How many stops away is the embassy?" Lana asked.

"Five," Mimi counted on her fingers, "including a transfer."

They paused in contemplation.

"It'd be dark down there. Pitch black," Lana said.

"We have a flashlight," Sam replied, "and we could get more."

"There are screen doors on the platform," Mimi said. "Suicide prevention doors."

"We could break the glass," Sam said.

"Has anyone seen the tracks? Do they have railroad ties? Would we eat shit?" Tyson questioned.

"I've seen the tracks," Mimi replied. "But what do you mean *eat shit*?"

"I mean, would we fall off the bikes? If so, we'd be better off just walking the tracks."

"I think we'd be fine," Mimi said. "It's like a sidewalk between the rails. Just concrete." A slab track.

"Are you sure? You got a good look at the tracks?" he asked.

"Yes. In Ilsan, the platforms don't have screen doors."

"Okay," Tyson said, "I'm in."

"We'll need a lock cutter and flashlights," Lana said.

"Bolt cutters," Tyson clarified, placing his hand on Lana's knee.

"And a hammer for the screen doors," Sam added.

"I'll ask Mrs. Jang what she has in storage," Mimi said.

∞

Mimi and Sam returned empty-handed but with word that the tools were in the maintenance room. They'd get them in the morning.

Mimi poked through the bag of food and cracked open a can of nuts.

"Can you pass the chips, please?" Lana asked.

"Sure." Mimi tossed them over.

Lana grabbed each side of the bag and pulled. "Ugh." The bag was stubborn, stuck.

"Let me try," Tyson said.

"I can do it," Mimi said. She took the bag, turned it sideways, pinched the corner, and ripped it open.

"Whoa. A life hack," Tyson said.

"You want some?" Lana asked, crunching on a chip. She held the open-faced bag out with both hands.

"No, thanks," Mimi replied. "I hate potatoes."

"Who hates potatoes?" Sam asked.

"I do." Mimi looked down at her feet. "I was on holiday from uni and hadn't seen my family in almost a year. My–"

"Oh, there's a story," Sam interrupted.

"My dad and I had rarely texted or talked while I was away, and I thought that we'd have some alone time, some quality time, that we'd do something special together. Instead, we had dinner with his business partner, and they talked about potatoes the whole time. Starting a potato liquor business. And all the while I sat there like a potato, not saying a word, wondering why I was even there, thinking he didn't care. When I got back to London, it seemed like every food was made of fucking potatoes."

∞

Room 317

Mimi and Sam took turns in the shower. She hopped in first and took her sweet time. A glamour shower. A Hollywood shower.

"Any hot water left?" Sam asked when she came out in a burgundy bathrobe. Her hair was a lustrous black, and she had a soft white glow to her.

"Oh, please. I wasn't in there that long."

"The fact that you're still alive means Mrs. Jang is right. The water's safe."

Room 315

Tyson sported an alma mater t-shirt—white, green, and orange with a logo of Sebastian the Ibis. An American white ibis. *Eudocimus albus*. According to Native American folklore, the ibis is the last animal to take refuge before a hurricane and the first to reappear afterwards.

Lana looked out over the street, breathing in the night air. She felt suffocated. Stuck inside. Waiting out the storm.

She felt Tyson's arms around her waist, him nuzzling her shoulder. Then, they were cheek-to-cheek. He kissed her jawline, took her by the hand, and led her to bed.

∞

Room 317

"Gotcha!" Sam swatted a mosquito with a three-day-old newspaper. The world's deadliest animal—killed by the world's second deadliest animal.

Mimi rubbed her eyes. "Thank you. Hopefully that's the last one."

He noticed the redness and swelling on her left arm. "Whoa. They loved you."

"And I hated them." She cleaned her bites with warm water and soap. "Mosquitoes are a nuisance I'll never get used to."

"So, tell me, do mosquitoes love some people more than others?" he asked.

"Scientifically speaking, yes. Twenty percent of people are especially attractive to them."

"So why are you a mosquito magnet and I'm not?"

"If I knew why, I'd try to change it. There are too many factors to consider. Chemical compounds in our skin. Carbon dioxide in our breath. Body temperature, sweat, perfume."

Sam yawned.

"Hey, you asked," Mimi said, noticing.

"I did. I'm just tired," he said with a sleepy face.

She turned off the light and he the lamp.

"Thanks for killing the mosquitoes," she whispered from her side of the bed.

"Anytime."

She crawled over and kissed him on the cheek. But the darkness hid his surprised smile.

Another mosquito lay in wait.

∞

The friends had the tools: bolt cutters, flashlights, and a hammer.

"Thank you, Mrs. Jang," Mimi said in Korean. "What do we owe you?"

"Nothing." She waved them off. "Just be safe and come back when you can."

"Thank you," Mimi said again. No promises.

Sam lifted his bag and looked through the tinted glass door. "Holy hell!" An approaching swarm of *gangshi*.

"They know we're here," Lana said. "They can sense us."

"Damn it," Tyson thought aloud. "What to do?"

Mimi uncrumpled the pink note from her pocket and ran through the list. "How about fire or mirrors?" she suggested.

∞

In the maintenance room, Mrs. Jang had enough wall and ceiling mirrors to build a fun house.

"I'll test one out," Sam volunteered, holding a round mirror to his chest.

Tyson reached for another.

"I've got this," Sam said to him. "Can you watch the door?"

"Are you sure?"

"Yeah." No overthinking this time.

Tyson cocked his head sideways. "If you insist. Be careful out there."

Sam stepped out into the sun and held up the mirror, and the *gangshi* hissed and moaned, hopping in all directions. In the blink of an eye, Sam saw mangled, greenish-white hands, a black bowl cut. {crash} Sam was bowled over on the asphalt. Blindsided. Pieces of glass pierced his palms and fangs tore into his torso.

"Stay here!" Tyson told Lana and Mimi. He grabbed a knife, pushed the door open, and lunged at the *gangshi*. Steel to skin. Blade to bone. The knife stuck to the *gangshi*'s skull, and Tyson toppled it over. Where the head goes, the body follows.

Sam was bloodied, disoriented, squinting at the sun. Tyson picked him up by the biceps and back of the head, donkey kicking a *gangshi* behind them.

"Walk with me," Tyson said, trying to hide his horror. He held Sam up and hurried him into the motel.

Lana and Mimi's voices were thick with emotion.

"Sam!"

"Mrs. Jang, the first aid kit!"

Tyson applied pressure to Sam's chest with a towel, Lana tweezed the glass out of his skin, and Mimi washed his wounds with warm water and soap.

Sam was trembling, shaking from his core. "It's just a mosquito bite," he murmured when Mimi neared his chest.

"Yeah." She smiled through her tears.

"I'm not gonna turn into a *gangshi*, am I? They're not contagious, right?"

"Right." Mimi put down the sponge. "You won't become one of them."

∞

Room 317

Sam was shivering, his forehead hot to the touch. Ibuprofen and his bed provided no comfort.

"What are you writing?" Lana asked him.

"A letter. A letter to my family," he stammered. "Can you give this to them if something happens to me?"

She eyed Sam's phone, avoiding his anguished gaze. "Yes, of course."

He exited the Notes app and pulled the covers over his face.

∞

Sam slumped over the two-seater table, his head cradled in the crook of his left arm. He cupped his bandaged hand over Mimi's soft hand,

and she caressed his thumb with hers. His fingers were frigid, his pupils dilated.

"Don't fade," Mimi said to him.

Sam had to consider every word he spoke, every inhale and exhale. Each spoken word was a dying breath.

He whispered, "*Gwaenchanha*." It's okay. I'm okay.

Sam waved Tyson and Lana over.

"How are you feeling, bud?" Tyson asked.

Sam shut his eyes and shook his head. He stretched out his free hand until his fingers touched theirs. And he felt warmth.

"Sam," Lana called out to him.

He lifted his eyelids, took one last look at Lana, Tyson, and Mimi, and squeezed their hands until his skin stung no more.

III

Room 315

"Burn in hell!" Tyson yelled, pushing a pillow out the window's ten-centimeter-wide opening. An anti-suicide window. The flaming, heart-shaped pillow fell on the *gangshi* below, eliciting shrieks and illuminating the street.

With a scowl on his face, Tyson gathered up the bed sheets, towels, and bathrobes. He was intent on burning the world to the ground.

{beep} Mimi and Lana stepped into the room and stared through puffy eyes at Tyson. He had a bathrobe in one hand, a lighter in the other. His own eyes were a dam of tears about to burst.

"Does fire work on them?" Mimi asked in a quivering voice.

"See for yourself," Tyson replied.

Mimi and Lana approached the window and arched their brows. The *gangshi* were fleeing the fire—as if they feared it—and the street.

"Give me those," Mimi said. She lit the bathrobe belt on fire and shoved the robe out the window, prompting the leftover *gangshi* to scatter.

From out the shadows, Sam's killer hopped into view with Tyson's knife still stuck to its skull.

∞

5:22 a.m. Sunrise. Mimi, Lana, and Tyson hadn't rested and digested. Their brains and bodies were adrenaline-fueled. In their hands they held the lighter and a makeshift torch (Mimi), the steak knife (Lana), and the hammer and a credit card (Tyson). Their bags were slung over their tear-soaked shoulders, with the bolt cutters, flashlights, and extra weapons within easy reach.

"Mrs. Jang," Mimi said, "please hold on to Tyson's credit card until we get in touch with Sam's family."

"Okay, I will," she answered as if money still mattered. "Will I see you again?"

"I hope so." Mimi paused. "We hope so." She took a deep breath.

"I'm really sorry about your boyfriend, Mimi. He died much too young."

∞

Mimi lit the torch, and its chemicals and fabric fast went up in flames. Higher and higher. Up and up. Could she and the couple reach Sinchon Station before the fire expired? she wondered.

{growl} Mimi pointed her torch at a couple of *gangshi* who looked like they'd died dieting. Emaciated. Emasculated. They angled their heads toward the shadows and hopped side to side, to and fro, figure-eighting.

{crack} Tyson interrupted the *gangshi*'s dancing with wild swings of his hammer. He connected with their necks and heads, exposing their brains.

Still, the *gangshi* were undead.

"Keep them distracted," Lana told Tyson and Mimi. She circled around the *gangshi* and stabbed them between the shoulder blades, and they fidgeted, froze up, and fell face forward onto the pavement, their stiff fingers snapping on impact.

"Why did that work?" Tyson asked as they ran downhill. His stare was intense, fiery.

"The lungs," Mimi said in between breaths. "Lana punctured their lungs, and they collapsed."

At the bottom of the hill, the trio ran right, past the police station and its unmoving flags, a red post box, and a row of abandoned food stalls with *tteokbokki*, dumplings, fish cakes, blood sausages, deep fried vegetables, skewered chicken, and hot dogs on a stick, all spoiled in the heat. Mimi passed her torch over the stalls, and the flies lived up to their name.

"Sinchon!" Tyson read the English sign board. Sinchon Station.

Lana tried the outdoor elevator—out of order—and then turned her attention to the bikes. A dozen or so. Chained to pedestrian guard rails and tree stakes. She chose the nearest bike, black and orange and foldable. Mimi stood by a silver mountain bike and Tyson a flat bar road bike in pastel blue.

They wiped the sweat off their faces and, with squinty eyes, scanned the area for *gangshi*. None in the immediate vicinity.

Tyson took the bolt cutters out of the backpack and went to work. Back bent. Biceps flexed. Wrists stiff. He cut through the blue bike's chain lock like butter.

"Keep an eye out for *gangshi*!" he yelled. The silver bike's U-lock clanged to the ground.

A swarm of six *gangshi* hopped closer and closer, and Mimi and Lana readied their weapons, flaming torch and bloody steak knife.

"Hurry!" Lana yelled back at Tyson.

He fumbled and wrestled with the last lock, which was a few millimeters thicker than the other two. He tried bolt cutting at different speeds and angles, but the U-lock did its job.

When the *gangshi* reached the guard rails, Tyson rose and raised the bolt cutters, ready to strike. But the guard rails did their job, too. The *gangshi* bounced on and off the rails, hissing and moaning as if frustrated with their inability to reach a higher plane, physical and spiritual.

"Try this bike!" Mimi pointed to a red hybrid bike with a thin chain lock, which Tyson cut with ease.

They pushed their bikes over the tactile paving and stopped at the subway stairs. All they could see was darkness below.

∞

With a running start, Tyson pushed the last bike down the stairs, and Lana followed its path with her flashlight. Like the other bikes, it predictably rolled and bounced on its tires before flipping and crashing onto its side. Unlike the other bikes, it didn't make it all the way to the bottom.

Mimi traded her flickering, fading torch for a flashlight and scissors. She leaned on the cold steel handrails to keep her footing, and Lana and Tyson followed her down the stairs.

A whiskerless white rabbit with long pink ears and beady black eyes greeted them on the basement floor. A fiberglass statue cut off at the hips. No cute bushy tail. They picked up their bikes and pushed them past a large potted plant—probably artificial—and columns covered with posters advertising English and Chinese *hagwon*s and their attractive tutors.

Rounding a corner, Lana was knocked to the ground. Her bike, knife, and flashlight went down with her, and she shrieked.

Tyson was terrified for his girlfriend. She was alone in the dark with a *gangshi*, and the time it would take him to run over would feel like forever to her—or so he presumed. He grabbed Lana's fallen flashlight, which pointed away from her, and shined it in the direction of her screams.

Through the beam of light, Tyson saw a pig pile: Mimi on top of the *gangshi*, the *gangshi* on top of Lana. Mimi had buried Lana's fallen knife deep into the *gangshi*'s back; Lana was on her back, her arms bloodied.

And Tyson's terror turned to rage. "Mimi, move!" He grabbed the *gangshi* by its hair, which he wrapped around his hand, and dragged its still, lifeless body away from Mimi and Lana. The *gangshi* had visible entrance and exit wounds, but Tyson took no chances. He bludgeoned the monster to the point of no return. He hammered the point home: No one person or thing was going to harm Lana or Mimi.

Gasping, Lana stood over her bike, hands on her hips, blood streaming down to her denim shorts. She looked up at Mimi and Tyson, swallowed hard, and whispered, "Thank you."

"I'm glad you're safe," Mimi whispered back.

"Are you?" Tyson asked, only half-whispering. "I mean, are you okay, Lana?" He flashed the light on her arms. Scratches. Claw marks.

"Yeah." Lana paused to collect her thoughts. "It didn't get close enough to bite me. It was strong, but I was able to hold its wrists and push it back long enough for Mimi to help."

They looked over at the dead *gangshi*, its stiff arms still sticking straight out, reaching out for life.

Tyson held Lana's bloody hand and whispered to Mimi, "Thank you."

∞

Tyson lifted the bikes and bags over the turnstiles, and he, Lana, and Mimi ducked under and duck-walked through. One at a time, they carried their bikes down to the subway platform and, more vigilant than ever, looked high and low for signs of *gangshi* activity—death and destruction.

The platform was empty, silent, black. They wheeled their bikes past a coffee vending machine, a trash bin, and a full-length mirror, which made them jumpy, and paused at a red box mounted on the wall. "Portable Emergency Light" its sign said in English. Flashlights. Three of them. Mimi, Lana, and Tyson had all feared running out of flashlight batteries. Now they each had a spare Portable Emergency Light.

At the end of the platform stood a locked metal cabinet full of khaki sacks. The English instructions on its glass panels said: "Wear a gas mask in an emergency of toxic gas attack, chemical, biological, or radioactive contamination" and "How to use CBR (Chemical, Biological, and Radiological) Gas Mask: BREAK - OPEN - PLUG IN - WEAR - PULL." BREAK the glass. OPEN the khaki sack. PLUG in the filter. WEAR the gas mask. PULL the mask tight.

"Can we use these?" Tyson whispered. "For the *gangshi*."

"I don't think gas masks would help," Mimi replied. "The *gangshi* would still be able to smell our breath or the carbon dioxide in our breath, wouldn't they?"

"Yeah, I would think so. Can we get on the tracks already?" Lana asked.

Tyson took another look at the gas masks. "Yeah, let's go."

∞

Seoul Subway Line 2: The Green Line, The Circle Line, The Hell Train. A hell of a place to be at rush hour. But for the time being, it was a haven.

Lana, Mimi, and Tyson tiptoed over the shattered glass of the suicide prevention doors and the steel rails of the slab track.

"Mimi, where are we going?" Lana asked.

"Chungjeongno. Three stations down. Then we'll transfer to Line 5."
The Purple Line.

They lined up their bikes back-to-back-to-back and pointed their
flashlights straight ahead, their weapons within arm's reach.

"Okay, keep a bit of distance. I'll flash my light if we need to slow
down, and if I yell, stop," Tyson said. He tugged on the front of his
shirt and the straps of his backpack, sticky with sweat.

They pedaled slow and steady down the center of the track, between
the rails, careful not to veer to the left or the right. It was almost
meditative—their intense visual concentration, the sounds of their
spinning spokes.

{slam} Something hit the platform screen door. Lana dropped her
flashlight. They braked their bikes. Tyson wielded his hammer.
Mimi aimed her light at the door.

A swarm of *gangshi* was on the other side of the glass. They scraped
the glass with their bloody claws and hit the door headfirst, the
sounds echoing through the tunnel.

"Let's go!" Lana yelled. She pulled the Portable Emergency Light
out of her bag and bumped her bike into Tyson's.

As they sped away, Mimi watched Lana and Tyson's shadows on the
wall and caught a glimpse of a green subway sign: Ewha Womans
University. Her uni.

∞

Mind the gap, Mimi thought. She and Tyson lifted Lana onto the
Chungjeongno Station platform, and they again tiptoed over shards

of glass. Without a *gangshi* in sight, they picked up their bikes and followed the purple subway transfer signs, whose arrows seemed to point toward hope.

Mimi, Lana, and Tyson went up a flight of stairs, then coasted down a long, winding corridor. They passed a pastry shop, a convenience store, and a blue metal cabinet before stopping at a stairway similar to an animal lair. Dark and cavernous. A cacophony of growls, hisses, and moans. A strange stench.

They hopped off their bikes and shined their lights on the *gangshi* scattered on the stairs. Eight in total. The *gangshi* stubbed their toes on the steps and toppled over. Over and over again.

"They can barely climb up," Mimi said.

"Good," Tyson replied. "This buys us time." He leaned his bike and backpack against the tiled wall. "I'll be right back."

"Wait, what? No. Where are you going?" Lana questioned.

He was already gone.

Mimi and Lana kicked their kickstands down and set their bags on the ground. They stood back to back in a defensive stance, beaming their flashlights around the corridor and stairway, watching, waiting, wishing for relief.

{smash}

"What the hell was that?" Mimi asked.

"Tyson!" Lana yelled.

They heard the clinking and crunching of broken glass followed by feet shuffling and running. The footsteps sounded closer and closer. They raised their weapons.

"It's me!" Tyson said a safe distance from the girls' knife and scissors. "Try these on." Gas masks in khaki sacks.

Lana grabbed him by the arm. "What is wrong with you?!"

"I…"

"Why would you just disappear like that? And here and now? Don't ever fucking do that again!"

"I'm sorry. I won't." He hung his head and could think of nothing else to say.

Wearing the gas masks, listening to their own breathing, the trio used the handrails until they were halfway down the stairs. They aimed their lights and weapons at the *gangshi* and stood in place. But the *gangshi* continued working their way upstairs, relentless as ever.

And Mimi knew she had been right. She took off her mask and spoke up, "It's no use. They still know we're here. They can smell us." She paused and took a step back. "But we have the advantage here."

∞

The *gangshi* faced an uphill battle. Halfway up the stairway they were blocked by a barricade of bikes, whose frames and spokes trapped and tripped them up. If the *gangshi* managed to get back on their feet before they got stabbed, Tyson hit them with his hammer and handlebars. When they lunged forward, he used his tires as shields.

Mimi and Lana dug their blades deep into the last *gangshi*'s lungs, securing a decisive victory for the humans. And Tyson grimaced and turned his head, retching and gagging.

"What's the matter?" Mimi asked, her hand on his shoulder.

"The *gangshi*." Tyson cleared his throat. "They smell godawful."

∞

At Seodaemun Station, a man's screams pierced the walls and doors, and the trio came to a screeching halt on the tracks. Yet no cry for help came. Perhaps the man's time had come; perhaps Mimi, Lana, and Tyson needed to save themselves. The darkness created a chasm between intention and action.

"Let's go on," Lana said with a hint of regret.

They pedaled away, paranoid and even more aware of the danger lurking in the shadows. A force so dark that it threatened humanity.

A ways down the track Tyson flashed his lights. They pumped, then squeezed their brakes and came to a complete stop.

"What is it?" Mimi asked him.

"A water break."

"Oh." Relief.

They shared the last of Mr. Shin's bottled waters, Jeju volcanic mineral water. No one had an appetite.

Tyson suggested that they consolidate their bags into one. "We'll need to be light on our feet."

"What supplies will we need?" Mimi asked. Flashlights, weapons, American passports, a Korean national ID card, credit cards, U.S. dollars, Korean *won*, phones, and chargers.

"What if the embassy is closed? What about this other stuff?" Lana asked. Food, clothes, towels, toilet paper, garbage bags, ibuprofen, and bandages.

"We need to think positive. The embassy will be open. And if, God forbid, it's not, we can come back for these," Tyson said, tossing aside a white towel.

"Mimi, you know the area. What should we do when we get to the station? How do we get to the embassy?" Lana asked.

"Hold our breath and run."

∞

A stalled subway train stood between them and the Gwanghwamun Station platform. Mimi, Lana, and Tyson stared at the train and then at their bikes, which they knew they had no choice but to abandon. On bare knees and elbows, they army-crawled on the slab track under the subway cars. The concrete was cold, hard, and unforgiving. From a hole in the wall, a little brown rat appeared, squeaking and scurrying alongside them. But it didn't frighten them. Better the devil you know.

At Exit 2 they took a deep breath and the path of least resistance, the sidewalk. To their left was a traffic-jammed Sejong Street. Cars, taxis, city buses, tour buses—all unmanned. In the median strip— Gwanghwamun Plaza—the bronze statue of Sejong the Great sat on his throne. A swarm of *gangshi* hopped aimlessly about the sculptures of the king's inventions—a sundial, a celestial globe, and the rain gauge—their chins, claws, and clothes covered in blood.

At their back, out of the trio's field of view, hundreds of *gangshi* surrounded the statue of Admiral Yi Sun-shin, savior of the Joseon dynasty. The 12.23 Fountain, commemorating the 23 battles Admiral Yi won with 12 warships, had become a literal bloodbath, with Seoulites and *gangshi* fighting tooth and nail, fang and claw. The *gangshi* had had a feeding frenzy.

The tired Tyson, Lana, and Mimi could only hold their breath and run for so long. It was lactic acid hell. They gasped for air, and the *gangshi* caught whiffs of their scent and hopped toward them.

Up ahead the trio spotted the waving Stars and Stripes, then it was an all-out sprint for the U.S. Embassy, past a caravan of Korean police buses, an array of potted flowers, and a high white wall topped with a metal security fence. They stopped at a closed gate and read the sign through blurry eyes: "Entrance for American Citizen Services."

"Let's hide our weapons," Tyson said, holding the drawstring bag open. Mimi and Lana took a look around before surrendering their scissors and knife. No *gangshi* was close enough to harm them.

Tyson pushed the buzzer on the wall, and Lana crossed her fingers.

∞

The drawstring bag passed through the x-ray machine, and the operators confiscated the weapons and gave Mimi, Lana, and Tyson the pat-down treatment.

At the end of the conveyor belt, a middle-aged man in a blue suit greeted them with a firm handshake.

"Hi, I'm Marty Whitmer. I'm a consular officer. You look like you've had quite a journey," he spoke diplomatically. They had bloodied clothes, baggy eyes, and hair stuck to their foreheads.

"I'm Lana." She extended her bandaged, mummy-like arm to shake his hand.

"Tyson." His palms were sweaty.

"Mikyung." Her nail polish was chipped.

Marty sat them down in an empty, sterile conference room, at a table big enough for twelve.

"I'll go get some water," he excused himself. He cleaned his hands with two squirts of hand sanitizer before fetching three bottled waters, a pen, and a notepad.

Tyson tapped his fingers on the tabletop.

"Are you Americans?" Marty asked when he returned. He sat on the other side of the table.

"We are," Lana said, pointing at herself and Tyson. "And our friend is Korean."

"Do you have your passports with you?"

"Yes," Tyson answered. He searched the drawstring bag.

"I have my ID card," Mimi said.

"Sure, please slide it over."

"Lana Maria Alvarez and Tyson Taylor," Marty read aloud and scribbled on his pad. "Do you reside in Korea?"

"We're, uh, visiting," Tyson replied.

"And Han Mikyung," he read in Korean. "From Goyang City. Ilsan."

"Yes. Do you happen to know how Ilsan is doing?" Mimi asked.

"The same as Seoul, I'm sorry to say," Marty replied.

Mimi buried her face in her hands.

"Mikyung, is your family in Ilsan?"

A muffled "yes." Puddles of tears formed in her palms.

Lana rubbed her friend's back, and Tyson opened the bottled waters.

"Okay, so here's where we're at," Marty said. "I don't know how you got to the embassy or why you didn't go to one of our ECCs. We–"

"What's an ECC?" Tyson cut him off.

"Evacuation Control Center."

"We heard about Mokdong and Jamsil," Mimi said, sniffling and wiping her eyes, "but we didn't think we could get there in time."

"Marty, please say that you can help us," Tyson cut to the chase.

Marty looked down at Tyson and Lana's dark blue passports—at the U.S. coat of arms emblazoned on the covers. The bald eagle, *Haliaeetus leucocephalus*, clutching an olive branch and arrows. An unsupported shield on the eagle's breast.

"I can help Lana and Tyson. A helicopter will be here at four o'clock to relocate you to Busan. From there, you'll be evacuated by boat to Japan and repatriated to the U.S." Marty turned his attention to Mimi. "And Mikyung, I'm trying to figure out what we can do for you. If you'll excuse me, I'll make some calls." He stood up and walked out.

They sat in stunned silence.

"Mimi, we'll get you on that helicopter," Tyson said.

She gulped.

∞

"We can't transport Mikyung out of Korea," Marty reported, "but we can relocate her to safety in Busan if…"

"Yes!" The trio smiled and embraced one other.

"Wait, wait, wait, there's a catch," Marty said.

Their spirits sank.

"This is the last helicopter to the embassy, and we don't have enough seats for all three of you. Embassy employees have priority."

"So what are you saying?" Lana asked.

"I'm saying that only two of you can go."

"You've gotta be kidding," Tyson said. "What's one more person?"

"We're at full passenger capacity and weren't expecting evacuees. As a matter of fact, the U.S. Embassy is only authorized to evacuate State Department employees."

"So you're bending the rules for us," Tyson said. "Can you bend them a little more?"

"No, I'm sorry. This is final."

"Can we talk to your supervisor?" Lana asked.

"Again, this is final. His words, not mine."

∞

"Marty, can we speak in private?" Tyson asked.

They stepped out into the hallway.

"You say that the helicopter is at passenger capacity. But what about cargo?"

"We've crunched the numbers," Marty replied. "Passengers. Cargo weight capacity. Weight distribution." He listed on his fingers.

"What cargo are you carrying?"

"That's classified information."

"Tell me what cargo is more precious than a human life."

"We have documents that could affect millions of people."

"And you can't save them to the cloud or a hard drive?"

"We need hard copies of certain documents."

"Like what?"

"Again, that's classified."

"Marty, there's gotta be a way to cut the red tape here."

"I'm afraid there's not."

"To cut the bureaucratic bullshit."

"Excuse me?"

"We're talking about a human life here."

"Tyson, I fully understand the scope of the situation, and your hostility won't help you or your friends. We have two seats available, and I'm not obliged to take any of you. Now, tell me, who's staying and who's going?"

Tyson leaned his head on the wall, to the left of a framed photo of smiling suits, American and Korean. The sans-serif caption read: "60 Years of Partnership and Shared Prosperity."

Beyond the wall, in the conference room, Lana and Mimi sat in a state of uncertainty, stuck in a man-made hell.

Tyson's throat tightened. "Lana and Mimi will take the flight."

"That's noble of you, Tyson." Marty softened his tone. "Chivalry is alive and well."

Tyson turned to face him. "It's not a matter of nobility and chivalry. Without the girls, I'd be dead."

Marty scratched his head. "I can give you my word that Lana and Mikyung will be transported to safety. My team is well-trained to handle this type of situation."

"Yeah, I'm counting on it."

"Very well. Now, I'll leave you to say your goodbyes."

"Wait..."

Marty stopped mid-stride.

"Do you have a pen and paper?"

Marty eyeballed Tyson with a mix of scorn and sympathy.

∞

Marty stood like a statue in the center of the room, and the trio walked over to him, taking their not-so-sweet time.

"When their uniforms are on, some men lose their souls," Mimi said just loud enough for the consular officer to hear. Lana nudged her side.

Mimi handed Tyson a hand-drawn, color-coded map back to Hongdae, and he hugged her. A hard hug.

He handed Lana two handwritten letters and kissed her on the lips. A hard kiss.

He took the weapons from Marty's hands and stared him down. A hard stare.

Tyson placed the knife and scissors in the drawstring bag, drew a deep breath, and walked through death's door.

IV

The black and white helicopter lifted off from the U.S. Embassy and turned south, away from Gwanghwamun, the main gate to the main palace of the Joseon dynasty, and Bukhansan, the highest mountain in Seoul.

Lana and Mimi sat squeezed between State Department employees and stacks of corrugated storage boxes. They didn't dare look out the windows for fear of seeing Tyson among the army of *gangshi*.

∞

Police and military manpower proved to be powerless against the necromancer's army of the undead. Hell had been raised, and the heavens had to intervene.

The summer sky became clear, cloudless. The sun overpowered the moon. And Mother Nature and Father Time came to collect their lost children.

The *gangshi* tried to shun the sun, taking refuge in the darkness, clinging to the shadows. But they couldn't hide from the torrid heat. Their stiff arms softened, their hands fell to their sides, and their fingers slid downward.

Their bodies bloated and exploded—food for stray dogs and cats.

∞

The stench of decay hung over the city. The past had come back to haunt Seoul, and memories of madness were scorched into the people's hearts and minds and souls.

∞

The double doors swung open, and Mimi and Lana stepped out into the sun.

"It was a breath of fresh air meeting you two."

"Yes, thank you for traveling all this way to see us."

"Please come visit us again. You're welcome here anytime."

"Say thank you to your families for the gifts."

They embraced one another.

Lana and Mimi exchanged a knowing look and dug into their purses.

"Wha-what are these?"

"Letters from your sons."

www.ingramcontent.com/pod-product-compliance
Lightning Source LLC
Chambersburg PA
CBHW030600130626
46552CB00006B/2613